The Things We've Seen

Speculative Tales from the Care Home Writing Club

by

Maggie Holman

Also by Maggie Holman:

'The Wishing Sisters'
'Footprints in the Snow'
'The Knocking'

*

'The Things We've Seen' © Maggie Holman 2021

Maggie Holman asserts the moral right to be
identified as the author of this work.
ISBN 978-90-820089-5-1

Cover design by Nik @ Book Beaver

To my dear old friends.
May you still find some
magic in the world
as we age together!

<u>Chapter 1</u>

"So, what d'you think she'll be like?"

"Young."

"Obviously. Students are usually young."

"Not always."

"A hippy."

"I don't think there are any hippies these days."

"OK. Punk, then."

"Maybe."

"Those other people, the ones who wear black all the time."

"Who?"

"You know, a Goth, like your grandson."

"Hope not!"

"Hey - what's wrong with my grandson?"

"I never said anything about your grandson!"

"Don't argue, you two!"

"Perhaps she'll be smartly dressed, business like."

"Maybe."

"Friendly."

"Better be!"

"Nervous."

"What, of us lot? Never!"

"Enthusiastic!"

"Now that's a big word for this time of day!"

"Don't tease."

"What's her name again?"

"Alice."

*

Just then, a knock at the door stopped their conversation abruptly and they all turned as one.

"Afternoon, everyone!" said Maureen, the day manager, as she opened the door and breezed in, "And how are we all today?"

Distracted murmurs of "Fine" and "OK, thanks" shot back at her, because everyone was more interested in the young lady at Maureen's side. She wasn't hippy, punk, Goth or smartly-dressed, but she did look friendly. She was dressed casually in jeans, trainers and a plain black T-shirt, and her dark hair hung loose over her shoulders. She stared straight back at the little group of five who were weighing her up and she weighed them up in turn.

Two ladies, one tall and elegant, the other more petite, sat on either side of a Scrabble game. One man sat by himself in one of the armchairs, reading a magazine. His long silver hair was pulled back in a ponytail and he was dressed, unexpectedly, in jeans and a T-shirt, on which was an image of a motorbike. Another man, dressed more like Alice's own Grandad in plain trousers and a shirt, sleeves rolled up, was sitting at the dining table, busy with a game of chess. His opponent was a third lady, small, round, her white hair pulled back in a bun. The only things they definitely had in common were their ages and their residential address. Otherwise, they seemed to be an interesting collection of diverse friends.

"So, Alice," Maureen continued, "here are our five lovely residents who want to take part in your writing project. We call them the Day Room Gang, because they're always in here together, chatting and making plans, and sometimes making mischief, right ladies and gents! They have some sort of special bond that our other residents aren't a part of. Not quite sure what it is!"

She turned to Alice.

"I'll leave you to get on with introductions and the things you want to talk about. I'll be in my office if you need anything. Have fun!"

With Maureen gone, there was a momentary pause, an awkward silence in the space between the old and the young.

"Well, don't just stand there," said the man with the ponytail, "Pull up a chair."

"Thank you," said Alice.

She sat down and pulled a notebook from her bag, aware of the five pairs of watching eyes. No-one spoke, so she began.

"Well, why don't we start by introducing ourselves? As Maureen said, I'm Alice, Alice Johnson. I'm doing a final-year project at the university about creative writing activities with the elderly."

"Why does it have to be about 'the elderly'?" said the lady chess player.

"Because people always think we're doddery and losing our marbles, and they think writing will keep our brains working," replied the man with the ponytail.

They all laughed.

"That's what everyone always thinks about us," said the tall lady.

Alice was suddenly embarrassed at alluding to the ages of her companions and made a mental note to respectfully never mention the word 'elderly' again.

"Anyway," the tall lady continued, "We interrupted. We're supposed to be introducing ourselves. I'm Daisy."

"And I'm Barbara, but everyone calls me Babs," said her Scrabble-playing friend.

"I'm Bill," said the man with the ponytail.

"I'm Harry," said the chess-player.

"And I'm Emma," said his partner.

"Thank you, everyone," said Alice, as she closed her notebook, "Now, Maureen has explained what my project is about, yes?"

"She said someone was coming to write stories with us," replied Emma.

"Did she explain what kind of stories?"

"No. You're going to do that, aren't you? It's your project," Babs piped up.

"Of course," said Alice, although she groaned inwardly, hoping that Maureen might have prepared the group a bit more, since she'd put a lot of detail in her email. "My studies are in Health and Social Care, and I'm interested in the effect that creative writing has on… imaginative thinking."

She paused, feeling less confident, and watched her audience as they mulled this over.

"You mean its effect on the *elderly*," Bill commented.

"Well, yes. I just didn't want to use that word."

"Which word?"

"Elderly."

"People always want us to write about our memories," said Harry.

"Yes," Emma joined in, "like about when we were kids or if we remember what happened in the war."

"Exactly," said Alice, feeling a bit more animated, "With this project, I would like to try something different, something a bit freer, and see what happens."

"So would we," said Bill, "Right, everyone?"

The group murmured in agreement.

"Well, Alice," said Daisy, "Come on. Spill the beans! What's the plan?"

"And I hope it's not too simple. I like a challenge," said Babs, "You can see we're all bright as buttons here; not a doddery brain cell between us."

"Of course," Alice continued, "So, I'm going to visit every Thursday afternoon for six weeks, starting this Thursday. We'll work together on some creative writing, and I'm hoping that by the sixth week, you'll all have a story to share."

"Easy!" said Bill.

"Ah, but wait," Alice announced, "there are three rules."

"Oh no! And they are?" Harry asked, in mock-concern.

Alice felt her confidence return and she relaxed. She looked at each of her group members, at Daisy, Babs, Bill, Harry and Emma. Yes, my dears, she thought to herself. I can be mischievous too, and I want to make sure you come along.

8

"You'll find out at our first session," she replied, "on Thursday afternoon."

Chapter 2

"So, what d'you think the three rules will be?"

"The stuff we're not allowed to write about, of course!"

"No sex!"

"Oh, behave!"

"No drugs."

"No rock'n'roll!"

"Great song, that."

"Yes, good old Ian Dury."

"Who's Ian Dury?"

"Never mind. Anyway, she said we weren't writing about our childhoods."

"Or the war."

"Thank goodness!"

"No swearing."

"I didn't swear."

"I mean, in our stories."

"Oh, yes. That's important."

"We don't swear. We're all well-behaved."

"We are! We just want to get on with it, right?"

*

Alice knocked on the door and walked into the Day Room. Her five elderly writers were gathered around the dining table, waiting expectantly.

"Hello, everyone," she said, pulling up a chair to join them, "How are you this afternoon?"

"Good, thanks," said Harry.

"Raring to go, right, gang?" said Babs, speaking for them all.

"Then let's go!" said Alice, as she pulled five brand new exercise books and pens from her bag and passed them around.

"Do we write our names on the front?" said Harry.

"It's like being at school," said Bill, "Which class are we in? Top set?"

Everyone laughed.

"Behave," said Daisy. "Let Alice get on with her project."

"Yes! We want to know what the three rules are!" said Emma.

"OK. Now," said Alice, "As I said already, this project is about writing fiction. You do know what I mean?"

"Making it up," said Babs.

"Exactly, so you're all going to write your own stories – I hope! – that you make up yourselves."

"How many words does it have to be?" said Bill.

"There's no word count," Alice replied, "That will just get in the way. I don't want you to feel under pressure. I want you to enjoy writing something. The story can be as long or as short as it needs to be."

"Daisy will write a lot. She's always writing in her diary or writing letters to people," said Emma.

"Hey, Daisy. Bet you were a right swot at school," said Bill.

"Will you stop it!" Daisy countered, "And let Alice get on with it!"

"Sorry, Alice," said Bill.

Alice was waiting patiently, allowing them their little banter.

"That's alright, and now, as you already mentioned, there are three rules."

They all leaned forward, intrigued.

"First, as we've discussed, it has to be fiction. Second, you have to put yourself in the story, but you don't write in the first person, you write in the third person."

"What does that mean?" asked Bill.

"It means you write from a 'he' point of view, not an 'I' point of view," said Daisy.

"Told you she was a swot," said Bill.

"And I told you to leave me alone!" said Daisy.

"Stop arguing, children!" said Babs. "What's the third rule, Alice?"

"It has to be a fantasy story. You know, have something 'unreal' in it, something that couldn't really happen."

Alice scanned everyone's faces. They seemed to be mulling over this third rule a bit more.

"Like a ghost story, for example?" said Bill.

"Could be," she replied.

"Or a story where you can do something or go somewhere or meet someone you know is impossible in real life?" said Harry.

"Yes, exactly, and so today, I thought we could all try out some little exercises, to get us into the swing of things."

"Not the rules we thought, then!" whispered Bill, winking at Harry.

"What's that, Bill?" said Alice.

"Nothing."

Alice opened her own notebook.

"Right, I've got an example here, of some writing that has me in it, but isn't in first person. Ready?"

They all nodded.

"Alice woke up early," she began, "She was excited. It was her birthday. There, see what I mean?"

They all nodded again. Alice wasn't sure they did understand.

"Now, can you all try the same thing? Write a sentence which has yourself in it, but in third person. Please ask if you need any help."

Everyone opened their new books. They began their writing at different times and in different ways. Babs began to write immediately. So did Daisy. Harry started something, stopped again, tore out the page, put it in his pocket and started again. Emma stared out of the window for a while. Bill hummed to himself while he doodled on the page. Eventually they all wrote something and put down their pens.

"It would be nice to share your writing," said Alice, fingers mentally crossed that they'd want to, "Who would like to go first?"

"I will," said Babs, holding her book up high. "Barbara was beautiful. Everybody said so."

They all laughed.

"It's good, Babs," said Alice, "You've got the right idea."

"And it's fantasy!" said Bill, winking at Alice.

Babs play-punched Bill's arm.

"Who wants to go next?" said Alice.

"Me!" Bill called out, "Here goes. Someone knocked on Bill's door and said 'Here's your new Ducati. You won it in a raffle,' and then he woke up. It was just a dream."

"What's a Ducati?" asked Emma.

"A motorbike," said Harry. "What else would Bill write about?"

"And it's another good example, Bill. Thank you. Anyone else want to share?"

Alice looked at her three remaining writers.

"Emma woke up with a headache."

"When Harry went to the shop, he bought a newspaper."

"Daisy loved her garden."

"Well, that was a great start," said Alice, "I think you're all good with writing about yourself in third person. Now, we're going to try another short exercise, writing something with yourself in it, but with a fantasy element. I've got my example here to show you."

"Fire away!" said Bill.

"The post arrived," she read, "There was a letter with a postmark and a stamp that Alice didn't recognize. When she opened the envelope, all it contained was a single sheet of blank paper, but as she stared at it, words began to appear on the page in front of her eyes."

"Ooh, I like that," said Babs. "Very mysterious!"

The others nodded and murmured in agreement.

"Thanks. Now, your turn."

Alice watched the group. She expected this task to be more of a challenge to their elderly minds, but to her surprise, they jumped straight in and wrote quickly.

"Babs knew that if he put this secret ingredient in his food, everything would get better."

"Bill's eyes must be playing tricks. How could someone he hadn't seen for more than sixty years suddenly appear, and not have aged at all?"

"Harry wished he could find a way through the snow and, miraculously, his wish came true."

"As Daisy was walking around the garden, a voice spoke to her from the flower bed. Did a *flower* just speak to her?"

"Emma went into the kitchen and discovered that it had changed. It looked the same as it did thirty or so years ago, before they had it renovated."

Everyone looked at Alice when the readings were finished. At first, she said nothing.

"Well?" said Babs, "Do you like our examples?"

"I love your examples," she replied. "They're great. They're.."

"Not what you were expecting, right?" said Bill.

"No. Not at all."

"So do we start writing stories next time?" Emma asked. "Are we ready? Did we pass?"

"Most definitely."

"Don't you worry, young lady," said Daisy, "We're going to do you proud for your university project!"

<u>Chapter 3</u>

"So, how's your story going?"

"Not saying."

"Ah! I was hoping to catch you out!"

"No chance."

"I'm not telling either, so don't ask."

"Mind you, I did find it easy to get started."

"Of course you did."

"We all did!"

"Go on. Let me read a bit."

"No!"

"Just the beginning!"

"I said no!"

"You're such a tease."

"No, I'm not, but you – you're annoying. You never give up."

"Wouldn't want to be any other way!"

*

When Alice arrived the following Thursday, Maureen was waiting for her and took her to one side.

"Hello, Alice. Can I have a quick word?"

Maureen led Alice into her office, where she sat down and motioned to Alice to sit down opposite. To Alice's surprise, since she was expecting something bad, Maureen was all smiles.

"I just wanted to say how pleased I am that you came here to do your writing project. I don't know what you said in last week's session, but the Day Room Gang are totally fired up by your idea. They've been sitting together down there all week, writing furiously in the books you gave them."

Alice inwardly breathed a sigh of relief. Nothing to worry about, then.

"That's great to hear," she said, "I was worried they'd find it either boring or too challenging."

"Oh, no," Maureen continued. "You've definitely inspired them to write, although I don't know what they're writing about. I've been told they won't show anyone their work; not the staff and not even each other, apparently. I told you they got together and schemed, in the nicest possible way, of course!"

"Well, I'll see if they'll let me take a look."

"Oh, and when you get there, you'll find there's a new member of the group. I hope you don't mind. His name's George. He only arrived here on Monday and he asked if he could join you."

"That's fine. Thanks for letting me know."

"He's had a tough time, although I'm afraid I can't share the details with you."

"Of course not."

"I'm hoping that him joining your project will help him to settle in."

"Me too. Right, well. I'll get going."

"Enjoy your afternoon."

"Thanks."

When Alice knocked at the Day Room door and went inside, everyone was already busy at the dining table. She took in the little group with one glance. Babs and Emma were sitting together. Daisy sat further along the table by herself. Bill and Harry sat at one end of the table, with someone Alice guessed must be George sitting between them. They were all talking and writing, but they stopped when Alice approached.

"Afternoon, everyone," she said, sitting down beside them. "And hello, George. Maureen said you'd joined the group. I'm Alice. It's good you've got your own book. I'm afraid I don't have one for you. I didn't know you'd be here."

"We got one for him. We're taking care of him," said Bill. "Don't worry."

George smiled but said nothing.

"So, how are we all this week?" Alice continued, looking around the table.

"Fine," said Babs, "Right, everyone?"

The others nodded in agreement.

"And I've just been hearing all about how busy you've been already, which is great. Would you like to share what you've been writing? Anybody want to read something out loud, or let me take a look?"

As one, George included, the group closed their books.

"Oh?" said Alice, in a half-serious half-teasing tone. "I guess that's a no, then."

"The thing is," said Daisy, "we all know what our stories are going to be about and we just want to get on with them by ourselves."

"And then we want to read them out to you in the last week," said Harry. "If you don't mind."

"And we want to keep them secret until then," said Emma, "from each other as well."

Alice looked at George, Bill and Babs.

"Interesting idea," she said, "And is that alright with the three of you too?"

"Yes," said Babs, "But if we do it this way, will it spoil your work for your project?"

Alice shrugged her shoulders.

"Not at all. I just introduced the idea to you. I mean, it's great you've made your own plans. I just don't know what I'll do for the next three weeks while you're busy writing. I guess I'll be a bit of a wallflower!"

"You can make the tea," said Bill, winking at her.

<u>Chapter 4</u>

For the next three Thursday afternoons, Alice joined her writers and, as Bill had said, provided tea, biscuits and background moral support. They kept to their word, and they wouldn't let her take even the tiniest peek at their books. They seemed content to be left alone and even George had settled into the task. Despite being so new, he'd quickly fallen in with the Day Room Gang and become their newest member. Now, however, they all sat apart, in their own little worlds, like individual satellites in orbit around the dining table. They wrote, read, crossed out, re-wrote and re-read their secret stories, until session six finally arrived; the week of the 'grand reveal'.

*

"It's here."
"Our big moment."
"Are you nervous?"
"Me? No!"
"I am, just a bit."
"You'll be fine."

"I wonder what Alice will think of our stories."

"I hope she doesn't mind."

"What?"

"What we've done."

"'Course she won't."

"It feels a bit sneaky. We've tricked her."

"Only a bit."

"She'll be fine."

After a previous discussion with the group, Alice had invited Maureen along, and each of her writers had invited one guest; they'd agreed that a larger audience might be overwhelming. The session had been moved to the evening, to enable the guests to be free to come along after work, and now the normally-quiet Day Room was buzzing with activity. Maureen served drinks and snacks, while Emma's Goth grandson, Paul, chatted with Bill's grandson, Michael. Michael was wearing a motorbike jacket and carrying a helmet, clearly following in his grandfather's footsteps. George's daughter, Mary, was there, and Babs's son, David. Finally, Harry's son, Mike, arrived at the same time as Daisy's daughter, Lisa, and the audience was complete.

Everyone gathered around the dining table, visitors at one end, the Day Room Gang and Alice at the other, creating a sense of an audience and a performance area. At seven o'clock sharp, Maureen stepped into 'management mode' and clapped her hands to get everyone's attention.

"Good evening, everybody, and thank you for coming along. As you know, we've been really lucky to have Alice with us for the last six weeks. She's a student on the Health and Social Care course at the university and she chose us to take part in her research project."

Bill turned and winked at Alice.

"Now that the project ends with this event," continued Maureen, "I'm not going to say any more. I'll hand you over to Alice and she can tell you all about it."

"Speech!" Bill called mischievously, and everyone laughed.

Alice stood up, paper in hand, pleased she'd planned some words in advance.

"Well, good evening, everyone. Thank you for coming. To give you some background, I was interested in carrying out a creative writing project, but I wanted to do something different, something that wasn't just about memories, because that seemed to be what a lot of writing activities were about when I did my research."

Alice hesitated a moment and looked around the table.

"Not that there's anything wrong with writing about memories, of course. I just wanted to give the group a different challenge. So, to sum up, everyone was asked to write a piece of fantasy fiction, and include themselves in it. Those were the rules."

"But no sex, drugs and rock and roll!" Bill called out.

"Grandad! Behave!" said Michael.

"To my surprise," Alice continued, "everybody said they wanted to keep their stories a secret until this evening, and so I have to admit, I have not had any part in what we're going to hear tonight, apart from introducing the plan, and I haven't read any of the stories either."

"They'll be great!" said Emma's grandson.

"And now, let's begin," said Alice. "Before you all arrived, the group agreed on an order of reading and here it is. Babs is going first, then Daisy, then Harry, Bill, Emma and finally, George. I hope you enjoy listening to the stories."

She turned to look at the members of the Day Room Gang.

"And I hope you enjoyed writing them. Good luck, everybody!"

Chapter 5

Babs's Story: 'The Most Marvellous Thing'

Arthur sat up in bed and winced at his Sunday morning tea. He knew his children meant well, trying to help after Edie passed away, but he just couldn't get excited about this new-fangled Breville machine. He was supposed to just sit up, switch it on and - hey presto! - an instant start to the day without even getting out of bed, but it just wasn't the same. The Breville could never recreate the familiar flavour of the tea which Edie made every morning for the last thirty-eight years.

Arthur had been alone for almost three months now, and it wasn't getting any easier. Tears sprang into his eyes again, as he allowed himself to look into the gaping hole in the world where Edie should be.

"We were lucky enough to get old together," he told himself. "Edie wouldn't want you to mope around like this, would she?"

To shake himself out of his negative mood, he got up, dressed and went downstairs. He made a slice of toast and munched on it while the kettle boiled, but sitting here only made Edie's absence even stronger. Their kitchen had always been Edie's favourite place in the house. She'd loved to prepare wonderful meals or experiment with new and challenging recipes. Cooking was such a passion for her that in recent years, after she'd retired, she'd even decided to study the ingredients of ancient foods and what they might have meant to those people of long ago.

Now all that effort was for nothing. The kitchen was empty. Did it miss its regular inhabitant, Arthur wondered? Could a room feel emotional loss in the same way that people missed each other. He also wondered whether Edie, wherever she'd gone, was also missing her kitchen, or if she was cooking in a new 'spiritual' kitchen. He found this idea strangely comforting and his mood lifted.

Just then, Arthur's eyes fell on the row of cookery books on the shelf above the range. For the first time ever, he lifted one down and started to thumb through it, stopping now and then at pictures of the meals he and Edie had enjoyed together. For three months, Arthur had drifted through his days without a sense of routine, picking at food when he felt inclined, pretending he was eating well so his daughter wouldn't fuss. Now he was struck by an idea. He could feel closer to Edie by having a go at recreating their favourite meals! Suddenly inspired, he spent the rest of the morning browsing through Edie's cookery books and her collection of handwritten recipes and notes.

A couple of weeks later, Arthur was in his local supermarket. He perused the Chinese ingredients, browsing his list, when someone gently touched his elbow.

"Hello, Arthur," said a familiar voice. He turned and saw Edie's sister, Barbara, her skin tanned from her winter break in Spain.

"Oh, hi, Babs," he said, giving her a hug.

"I just got back. I was going to call you. How've you been, Arthur? Are you OK?"

Arthur's lip trembled and his eyes filled with tears.

"Let's go for a coffee across the road," Barbara whispered. "It's quieter there."

They sat down in a corner of the cosy olde worlde café. Barbara waited while Arthur stirred his coffee and put down his spoon.

"Well? You didn't answer my question."

He sighed and looked out of the window.

"Well, to be honest, I feel like I'm just drifting. I don't know where I'm going. Did you feel like this after you lost Peter?"

"Of course," Barbara replied. "It was a huge adjustment. One minute we were doing everything together, and the next he disappeared. I missed him terribly, and I had to make a whole new set of plans without him."

"I was thinking of calling you, actually. I've been working my way through

Edie's recipes, trying to recreate some of her favourites. I was going to invite you over for dinner."

"Which would be lovely, Arthur."

"Except," he continued in a mournful tone, "I certainly haven't got Edie's knack for throwing things together. I thought it would make me feel closer to her, but I don't know if it's working."

Barbara reached over and patted Arthur's arm.

"Then let's have that dinner very soon. What about Friday at eight? We can keep it simple; mince and dumplings. and I'll do the shopping."

*

On Friday, Barbara rang the doorbell at eight on the dot; she'd lost none of her regimented punctuality with age. Arthur took her bag of shopping and carried it through to the kitchen.

"Right then. Here we go. Mince, gravy, carrots, onions, flour, suet," Barbara said methodically as she spread everything out on the worktop. "Well, don't just stand there gawping. Come and help!"

Arthur put on some relaxing classical music while he and Barbara chatted about their week. He'd always got on well with his sister-in-law and he enjoyed her company. Together they chopped the onions and mushrooms, fried the mince and added the stock, but before they mixed the flour and suet for the dumplings, Barbara suddenly stopped what she was doing. She turned to Arthur.

"Right," she said, wiping her hands on a tea towel. "It's time to share something with you."

"Oh?"

"I want to add," she paused mid-sentence, "a particular ingredient to our dinner."

"What sort of ingredient?"

"Well, what would you say if I told you that I don't miss Peter as much as I used to, because Edie gave me something to put in my food, for whenever I was feeling upset or agitated about him."

Arthur's jaw dropped. Edie had never mentioned any of this to him.

"Did I hear you right?"

"You heard me."

Arthur leaned against the worktop. Barbara looked straight at him, deadly serious, and he knew she was telling the truth. He cleared his throat.

"So – how does it work?"

"You just add it to whatever you're cooking, of course! Weren't you listening just now?"

"That's it? And then what happens?"

"It's a bit difficult to explain. Here."

Barbara rummaged around in her handbag, pulled out a small, re-sealable plastic packet and passed it to Arthur. Inside he could see a fine powder, deep red in colour. Cautiously, he tucked a fingernail in the seal and prised it open. When he smelt it, the aroma was pungent and unfamiliar.

"You're joking, aren't you?" he said, laughing nervously.

"No, I most certainly am not. This is no joking matter! Now, you just sprinkle a little bit into the dumpling mix, and then we'll stir it in and add the water."

"I dunno, Babs. What's it going to do?"

"Well – I find it makes me a little sleepy at first, a little 'spaced out', as my grandson would say."

She held onto her head and swayed around a bit, laughing, but Arthur didn't laugh with her.

"You mean it's a drug," said Arthur, "What kind of drug?"

"Oh, I dunno. It's from South America, I think. I forget its name, so I just call it 'that red stuff', but don't be such a prissy-pants, Arthur! Edie helped me, and now I want to help you."

"Sorry, it's just, this is a bit weird."

Barbara smiled.

"Come on, let's do this. It's alright, really. I'll take care of you. Cross my heart."

Arthur sprinkled some of the powder onto his hand, tipped it into the mixing bowl with the suet, flour and water, and stirred while Barbara looked on.

"Hmm, a little bit more, I think," she commented.

He sprinkled more until Barbara seemed satisfied, then he added water, placed the sticky dumpling dough into the mince and put the dish in the oven.

The job done, Arthur felt apprehensive. He poured two tumblers of whiskey and he and Barbara played a couple of hands of rummy while their meal cooked. Finally, Barbara lifted the dish from the oven and divided its contents onto two plates. Arthur looked at the food. It certainly didn't look or smell any different. There was no sign of 'that red stuff' at all.

They sat at the dining table, turned out the lights and ate by cosy candlelight, but after a few minutes, Barbara suddenly put down her cutlery. She leaned forward on her elbows and put her head in her hands.

"Babs? What's wrong? Are you OK?" Arthur asked, reaching over to her.

When Barbara looked up again, she had a wistful expression on her face. She gazed past Arthur, but when he turned around to look, he saw nothing.

"Babsy?" he whispered.

Still Barbara didn't answer. Instead, she pushed her chair back, walked through to the conservatory and sat down on the window seat. After a moment, Arthur stood up to follow her. He was so surprised by what he saw that he hung back by the door.

He recalled the times Barbara and Peter used to visit, how they liked to sit together in this exact same spot, looking at the garden. Now, as Arthur watched, Barbara's lips moved. He was too far away to hear anything, but as she spoke, pausing now and then and nodding her head, he realised she was deep in conversation, with someone Arthur couldn't see.

Suddenly, he felt invasive. He stepped back into the dining room, and just then the walls seemed to blur and disappear from view. The lights flickered a few times and dimmed. He felt the same swaying feeling he'd once felt on a stormy ferry trip and he quickly made his way back to his chair. When he leaned against the dining table for support, it felt warm and pliable in his hands, instead of hard and smooth.

"What's happening?" he cried out. "I don't like it! Help me, Edie! Edie!"

As if in response, two hands touched his shoulders from behind, smooth, small hands, hands he knew well. He froze, confused, and then he felt someone lean into him and put their arms around his neck. A gentle forehead rested on his shoulder. He closed his eyes.

"Arthur," said a whisper in the background.

"Edie?" he choked. "Is that you? I'm scared!"

"Yes, Arthur, it's me. Don't be afraid. There's nothing to worry about."

Waves of grief and relief washed over him. He reached up and held onto the invisible encircling arms.

"Oh, Edie, I miss you."

"I miss you too, Arthur," the whisper passed near him like a breeze.

"And I'm so sad without you."

"But there's no need to be sad," came the whisper again.

"Don't let me go."

"I'll never let you go, my darling, not now that Babs has helped you to find me."

*

Someone was shaking Arthur awake. A voice invaded his dreams, whispered his name, but this time it wasn't Edie's. He sat up, suddenly alert, and stared into the concerned face of his sister-in-law. He looked around. He and Barbara were alone. It was dark. The candles they'd lit earlier on the dining table had burned away. Barbara turned on a light.

"I made some coffee."

Arthur sipped at the offered mug. The coffee tasted bitter and strange.

"You were talking to Peter," he observed.

"I was," Barbara whispered, and she paused, "Well? Did you see her?"

"I didn't see her, but I felt her. She held onto me, Babs, and she whispered to me."

Barbara's hands flew to cover her mouth, held back her gasp of joy.

"Oh, Arthur, I'm so happy for you."

Arthur looked at Barbara.

"What just happened to us?"

She shrugged her shoulders.

"I'm still not sure myself. All I know is that after Peter died, Edie suggested I try using this powder. She said people in the old days believed it had special powers. Whatever it is, it works for me, Arthur. I feel better, knowing I have a way back to Peter whenever I need it."

Arthur shook his head, still confused.

"She was really here?"

Tears filled his eyes.

"I think so," said Barbara, "and you know something, Arthur? No more tears, eh? We need to enjoy this moment, not weep. Look at the gift Edie's given us. You should be happy, not sad, that now she can be here whenever you want her to be. Isn't that just the most marvellous thing?"

Chapter 6

Daisy's Story: 'In My Garden'

Daisy was pretending. Every time she spoke to someone on the phone or replied to an email, she told them she was fine. She smiled gratefully to the volunteers who delivered her groceries and she waved to the neighbours from her window. She spoke to her daughter, Lisa, every evening, to touch base and to read instalments of her favourite children's books to Lisa's daughter, Lois. To the outside world, she was the same old Daisy, but inside, she was beginning to feel empty. With no-one to talk to for long periods at a time, Daisy began to talk either to herself, or to the things around her.

"Mad old bat!" she thought, "What would anyone say if they could hear you?"

Every morning, Daisy went out into the summer sunshine via the French windows of her South London town house. She crossed the patio, took hold of the handrail with her gnarled arthritic hands, walked gingerly down the concrete steps and set off across the lawn.

The garden was kept apart from the outside world by high red-brick boundary walls, and over the forty years Daisy had lived there, she was the one who'd lovingly created this hidden gem, and so she felt it was reasonable to say hello to every blossom, every leafy shrub, every grand tall tree, because really they were like old friends.

The garden was long and narrow, just like all the others in the terraced street, and on this particular morning, Daisy decided to wander down the path which snaked through it. She walked slowly and carefully, because her age required it, until she came to the low brick wall which separated the landscaped section of the garden from the wild flower garden at the end.

This unkempt meadow-like expanse was Daisy's favourite part of the garden, and she loved to survey her mish-mash of cornflowers, kingcups, forget-me-nots, daisies and columbine, the cow parsley, poppies and foxgloves and the ivy and honeysuckle which wound their way up the walls like a theatre backdrop. Every plant was Daisy's contribution to the welfare of the bees, butterflies and other insects and, unlike the landscaped section of the garden, she'd left it alone to grow in gay abandon in whatever way it fancied.

She sat down on the wall for a moment, a little out of breath, and was surprised at just how overgrown the wild flower garden had become. Gay abandon was all very well, but creating a space which enabled the torture and strangulation of the floral world was quite another. Making her way through to the back gate would be a bit of a challenge, as tendrils, plant roots and grasses had tangled themselves around each other across the path, creating a veritable death trap for her unsteady feet.

"Well, I hadn't noticed just how overgrown you'd become!" she said out loud.

"Then it's about time you got down here and tidied it up a bit," said a voice, "It's turning into a jungle down here. It's positively dangerous!"

Daisy lost her balance at the unexpected reply and almost fell off the wall in fright. She waited, but no further words came. The gentle breeze blew across the silent flowers. She looked around. Who just spoke to her? A neighbour, watching out of their window, to poke fun at her garden neglect? A passer-by in the back lane peeping through the gate to play a trick? Or did she imagine she just heard a voice, because she was a mad old bat after all?

"Hello? Hello?" she finally called out, tentatively.

"Hello? Hello?" mimicked a sing-song voice.

Daisy looked around quickly. She was confused. No-one was there. She was definitely alone.

"I expect you're wondering where I am?" said the voice.

"I expect I am," said Daisy.

"Look down here, a little to your left."

"It looks like I really am having a conversation with a flower!" thought Daisy, "How can that be?"

She leaned forwards and to the left, as instructed, and peered into the tangle of grass, ferns and blooms. At first, she saw nothing out of the ordinary, but then, as she watched, the plant stems close to the ground began to move. A tiny foot stepped out, and Daisy gasped and watched, transfixed, as two equally tiny hands took hold of the flower stems, pushed them back, and a little man stepped out. He stood there, hands on hips, and stared up at Daisy.

She stared back, open-mouthed. The little man was human-like, a perfectly-formed, scaled-down figure, with a bit of a pot belly. He was about six inches tall, with red hair and a wisp of a red beard, and was dressed in trousers, boots and a jacket that were clearly cobbled together or hand-made, and which bore the dust and mud of time spent outdoors.

"Are you a Borrower?" Daisy asked, thinking immediately of the book she'd just been phone-reading to Lois.

"Well, that's a new one," said the little man, "So, you don't think I'm a gnome, then?"

"I don't know. Are you a gnome?"

"I most certainly am not, not a gnome or a 'borrower', whatever that might be!"

"Then what are you?"

"I'm just plain old me! Let me introduce myself. I'm Rolf," he said, and he bowed graciously, "and I live at the bottom of your garden."

He stepped closer to Daisy and offered a tiny hand for her to shake. She took it between the tips of her forefinger and thumb, and shook it gently. It felt warm and soft, real. Daisy wasn't dreaming.

"I'm Daisy," she said.

"I know," replied Rolf, and then he began to laugh.

"You do know we shouldn't be shaking hands," he said, wagging his finger in reprimand, "what with social distancing and all."

"Oh, you know about the corona virus?"

"Of course. Doesn't everybody?"

"Yes, I know, but it's just that, you're…"

"Not human? Little? Live in a garden? You're right, I'm all those things, so you think I don't need to be aware of what's going on in the human world, or that I won't be affected by your human diseases?"

"I'm not sure what to think," said Daisy. "I'm struggling to believe you're real, even though I just shook your tiny hand."

"Oh, I'm real alright, as real as you are. Anyway, back to the virus. I was supposed to go on a trip to see my sister, Nancy, for a few days, but.."

"You have a sister?"

"Yes, I have a sister!" said Rolf, his tone a little tetchy. "Now will you please stop interrupting!"

"Sorry."

"She lives in a garden over in Maida Vale, belongs to another old lady, actually, but when I watched the news unfolding about Covid-19 and how dangerous it is for the elderly, I thought I'd better stay put. Nancy's my older sister, and she's quite a bit older than me, you see."

"How old is she?"

"Two hundred and four."

"Oh my, that's old! And how old are you?"

"I'm a hundred and seventy-six."

"Well, you certainly don't look it! Anyway, how did you manage to find out about the corona virus, if you live in my garden?"

Rolf paused.

"Well, sometimes I sneak into your house and watch the television."

He seemed a little embarrassed.

"You do? How come I never noticed you?"

"I'm very discreet."

"But how do you get into the house?"

"You do ask a lot of questions, don't you? Have you already forgotten how small I am? I can get through all sorts of holes and nooks and crannies and cracks."

"Well, I suppose you haven't been doing any harm by watching my television, but have you been anywhere else in the house?"

"No! I'm not a burglar! I just like to keep up with what's going on in the world, and watching your television is the easiest way to do it. Being this small has its disadvantages, you know. Imagine me trying to buy a newspaper!"

Daisy stood up, so that Rolf seemed even smaller.

"Well, I suppose there's no need for you to sneak around, now that we've finally met each other. Would you like to have some lunch?"

"Why not? After you!"

*

Daisy set off back towards the house, shuffling in her usual slow way, while Rolf marched along beside her. He needed to walk quickly, since his stride was so small, but still he got left behind. Now and then he had to do a few little running steps to compensate for this difference and catch up. When they reached the patio, Daisy stopped.

"Should I lift you up the steps?" she asked.

"Oh no, thanks. I'll meet you up there."

With that, Rolf turned right and headed over to the brick boundary wall, which was covered in thick, ancient ivy. He took a run, jumped up and grabbed onto a low-lying vine, and then nimbly pulled himself upwards, as if he'd done this a hundred times. When he was level with the patio, he jumped back down, did an entertaining stunt roll and ran across to where Daisy was standing.

"Beat ya!" he shouted, out of breath, as Daisy ambled up the steps to join him, "but I definitely won't be able to get onto one of your patio chairs. Can you lift me up onto the table and I'll sit there?"

"I can do better than that," said Daisy, after she did as he asked. "Just wait there."

In the spare bedroom which Lois used when she came to stay, Daisy went over to the doll's house in the corner. She took out one of the tiny china cups, a saucer, a plate, a knife and a fork, along with one dining chair and the dining table. After all, Lois wouldn't be playing with them for a while.

"Woah!" said Rolf, when he saw Daisy's collection of tiny household things, "Thank you! You're really spoiling me!"

Daisy made herself a cheese sandwich and a cup of tea, and she also cut up some tiny pieces of bread and cheese. She poured a few drops of her tea into the doll's house cup so Rolf had a drink too.

When they began to eat, Rolf was able to sit up at the little dining table and munch his own tiny pieces of food.

"This is nice," said Daisy.

"Hmm," Rolf agreed, between bites.

"So, what do you usually do for lunch? I mean, what do you eat and where do you eat it?"

Rolf smiled.

"There you go with your questions again! Should I just tell you all about my life in your garden, in one go?"

"Yes, please. I'd like to hear about it."

Rolf leaned back in his chair and put his hands behind his head.

"Well, I don't usually sit down formally like this. I usually just eat when I feel like it. When I'm feeling hungry, I go out and look for something. Mostly I forage about for things, like berries and mushrooms, or the apples from your tree. I have to wait til they fall on the ground and go soft. I can't climb trees easily, although I can get up to your strawberries!"

Rolf had a mischievous twinkle in his eye and Daisy laughed.

"I was sure I'd put them up high enough to escape the slugs and I couldn't understand how they'd still managed to nibble at them. Now I know!"

"Oh yes, that was me!"

"What about at night? Where do you sleep?"

"I have a special place I climb up to at night, a little hole high up in the wall. I love living in your garden, but it can be a bit dangerous for someone as small as me, so of course I can't sleep on the ground. I always have to watch out for rats and mice, and cats, of course, and there's a particularly nasty hedgehog I fell out with recently. He doesn't like that I live on his night-time route, but I keep telling him I was there first. I'm not scared of any of the animals, just careful. I'm not scared of anything, actually. I'm well-trained, see."

"Oh?"

"Yes. I'm a black belt."

"In karate?"

"No, silly, in archery!"

Rolf lifted the corner of his jacket to reveal the tiniest bow and a quiver of arrows, attached to his belt.

"In my world," he continued, "there are archery masters who train us all to use bows and arrows. They're our only real means of defence. When I was younger, my parents sent me to the local archery school. Black belt is the best you can be."

"Just like karate."

"Alright, if you say so! Anyway, I've seen off quite a few rodents and cats in my time. They haven't got me yet. My arrows are tiny but they're very, very, VERY sharp!"

Daisy sat quietly, mulling over this information.

"Got any more questions?"

"Yes. Have you always lived in my garden?"

"No. I moved in about ten years ago."

"Why?"

"It was vacant."

"No, it wasn't. I live here!"

"I know, but I mean it wasn't being used by any little people. I acquired the land rights from the Municipal Registry of Homes for Tiny People. I have a certificate to prove it."

"I'd like to see it."

"I bet you would, but you'd need a turbo-charged magnifying glass to read it."

"So, are there little people in everyone's garden?"

"Oh no, that's not how it works. We only move into the gardens of people who live alone."

Daisy calculated. Rolf said he'd been living in her garden for about ten years. It was ten years since her husband, Tom, had passed away.

"But what's the purpose of you being here?"

Rolf shrugged.

"Just to keep an eye, in case you need somebody. That's why I spoke to you this morning. It seemed like the right time for you to have some company, now that the corona virus has stopped you meeting everyone else. Besides, I'm more fun to talk to than the flowers. I can answer you back!"

*

Over the next few weeks, Daisy and Rolf met every morning in the garden and spent the day together. Rolf was full of ideas and Daisy was happy to indulge him.

"Let's have a race around the garden. Keep us fit!" he'd say, and they'd set off on an agreed amount of circuits, evenly matched as athletes because Daisy's large steps were frail and slow, while Rolf had little legs and more running to do, but he was fitter and faster.

"Let's play hide and seek!" was another of his favourites, and it was always Rolf who went to hide, since it was he who had an endless number of hiding places.

They improvised ways to play games together. They played skittles on the lawn, using Daisy's plastic egg cups and a ping-pong ball. They collected some tiny stones, small enough for Rolf to lift, and painted one set red and one green, so they could play tic-tac-toe on a chalk square on the patio. Sometimes they spent hours working as a team to clear the wild flower garden. Rolf shimmied up the plant stalks to snap off the old flower heads and pulled out all the dead grass and ferns, which saved Daisy from bending over and hurting her back. Her job was to rake everything up and make a bonfire, which they then used to cook baked potatoes for supper. Their newly-entwined lives were very busy, but sometimes, between all this busyness, they would just sit for hours, talking or watching the sunset, or Daisy would read her latest choice of book out loud, and Rolf would sit beside her, listening with his eyes closed.

Every evening they made sure they watched the BBC's Six O'clock News together, to follow the progress of the corona virus and the lockdown, which all seemed a million miles away from their contented garden world. Later, Rolf always said goodnight and slipped off to his sleeping place in the garden wall.

"You know you can always stay here inside the house," Daisy said on countless occasions, but he always refused.

"Thank you, but no. I need to stay out there and keep my skills sharp!" he would say.

One evening, Rolf was still sitting on the sofa with Daisy when her daughter called.

"Hi Mum. How are you?"

"Hello Lisa. I'm fine."

"Are you sure? You've been on your own for so long now. Everyone's starting to talk about the effect this is having on people who are stuck at home by themselves. I wish we could meet up."

"I know, dear. So do I, but I've been keeping myself busy. Don't you worry."

Daisy looked across at Rolf, who winked at her.

"And I wish you would try Zoom or Skype or WhatsApp or something," Lisa continued. "We'd feel closer then. We could see you while we chat."

"You know I like things as they are. All that tech stuff is so confusing! Listen, I have to go. I'll call later and read the next Harry Potter chapter to Lois."

"OK. Bye for now. Love you!"

"Love you too!"

When Daisy sat down again, she noticed that Rolf was looking a little sad.

"Are you alright, Rolf?"

"Yes, I'm fine, but I was just thinking about Nancy, and wondering if she's alright."

Daisy tried to put herself in Rolf's shoes. She didn't realise quite how lonely she'd been until Rolf said hello that morning in the wild flower garden. The corona situation was frightening and unknown, but at least Daisy could communicate with her family and friends by phone and email. She knew they were all safe and in turn, they knew she was safe, but Rolf and Nancy didn't have that kind of contact. Poor Rolf had been working hard to make Daisy's empty life so full of fun, when all the time, he had no idea if his own sister was safe.

"Rolf," she said, leaning forwards to get closer to her little friend, "Why don't we see if we can find a way to check on Nancy? Do you know the address of her garden? We could go there."

"But you're not supposed to go out of the house or meet people, Daisy. You're old, Nancy's old, I'm old. We're all old. What are we supposed to do?"

"I could ask my daughter to pop by."

"Really? You want to tell her about me? Would she believe you?"

"Good point, but at least think about it."

"OK. I'll think about it, if it makes you feel better."

Unfortunately, events conspired which would prevent Daisy and Rolf from making any further plans. That night, there was a garden invasion. They came over the wall from the back lane, hidden by the shadows, looking for spoils. The first Daisy knew of it was when the sound of breaking glass woke her suddenly. She peeped out of her bedroom window and saw a torch beam flickering around beside the potting shed. The night was warm, her window was open, and Daisy listened to the voices which travelled across the darkness; young male voices, two of them, teenagers, chattering conspiratorially. She was just debating whether to call the police, since really there was nothing worth having in the shed and the boys would probably just leave again, when a cry of pain shot across the night.

"Ow! What was that?" said a voice.

"Be quiet!" hissed the other.

"But I just got bitten or stung or something and it bloody hurts!"

"Stop being a wuss. It's probably just a mosquito or something. You'll wake everyone up with your…ow!" came a shout of pain from this voice too.

In seconds, both boys began to scream and yelp. The torch beam jumped around erratically as they twisted and turned, trying to avoid something which attacked them again and again from all directions, something unseen which they believed was stinging or biting them, causing tiny pin pricks of excruciating pain.

When Daisy worked out what was happening, she laughed out loud. She watched the torch beam move down the garden, as the boys made a run for it, escaped over the wall and disappeared down the street. Daisy blew a kiss into the garden to her invisible little hero, who had thwarted her night-time visitors, and she looked forward to laughing with him about the whole event when they met in the morning.

However, Rolf didn't appear when Daisy went to their usual rendezvous. She waited for a few minutes and then wandered around the garden, calling his name. She searched in the wild flower garden, underneath the hedges and shrubs and behind the large tree trunks. She looked high and low along the brick boundary walls for the little hole that was his sleeping place, but she was unable to find him and she was frightened. For three days Daisy searched frantically for her little friend, unable to settle or sleep properly, wondering where he was, unable to share her concerns with anyone. She was beside herself with worry.

She found him on the morning of the fourth day. He was lying at the foot of the boundary wall, on his side, breathing badly. Now and then his chest gave way to a violent coughing fit. Daisy knelt down beside him.

"Oh, Rolf. I've been looking everywhere for you! What's the matter?"

"You know what's the matter, Daisy. Stay away."

The teenage would-be thieves had run off empty-handed, with only a few pinprick bruises and their bruised pride, but Rolf had not escaped their visit. They'd brought something far more serious with them, from the world outside.

"I'm sure it's corona," said Rolf, between gasps for breath, "Probably mild, but enough to get a little guy like me."

Daisy burst into tears.

"Then we have to get you to a hospital," she cried.

"No, Daisy. You mustn't take any risks. I can deal with this myself. You have to keep away from me for fourteen days, like they tell you to on the news. I'll stay in the garden, and then you can come and find me."

"No, no, no, no, no! I want to help. You can't stay there, on the ground, so weak. You can't defend yourself if you can't use your bow and arrows."

"But you must think of yourself and your family now. You mustn't get sick."

"And you must think of Nancy, and get well!"

Daisy rushed into the house and back upstairs to the doll's house. She took out the little wooden bed, with its pillow and blanket. In the kitchen drawer, she found the gloves and mask which Lois had insisted on leaving with her at the start of the lockdown. She began to cry hot, heavy panicked tears as she pulled them on and rushed back outside.

She put the bed high up, at her own eye level, on one of the wooden shelves in the potting shed, then she went back to the kitchen and put some bread, cheese and berries on the doll's house plate. She filled a normal-sized saucer with water and took the doll's house cup so Rolf could help himself to a drink, and then she took everything out to the shed on a tray, left it by the bed and went back to find him.

"I'm going to make you a bit more comfortable and safe, little friend," Daisy whispered, and she knelt down, gently lifted Rolf in her gloved hands and carried him to the shed.

"Thank you," said Rolf, as he lay down on the bed and pulled the blanket over himself. "Goodbye for now, dear Daisy. See you in two weeks."

*

For the next two weeks, every moment dragged by. Daisy fretted and paced around the house and through the garden. She sat on the patio, lonely and scared, and stared at the shed. She stood outside it, at a distance, hoping and praying that Rolf was getting better inside. Daisy had no-one to talk to, no-one to share her worries with. After all, who would believe her?

"What's that?" they would say, as she played out the conversation to herself, "You just met a little man who's been living at the bottom of your garden for the last ten years and now he's caught the corona virus? Really? Mad old bat!"

The minute Rolf's self-quarantine was over, Daisy hurried to the shed as quickly as her frail legs would carry her, threw open the door and rushed inside. The shed was silent. It smelt empty. It felt empty. It *was* empty. Rolf was gone. The early morning sun shone through the still-broken window. Flecks of dust danced and played in its soft light. As they settled, they landed softly on Rolf, on his motionless body lying in the doll's house bed. One of his tiny hands peeped out from under the blanket and hung limply over the bedside. Daisy gently touched it. It was porcelain white and porcelain cold. She went back outside and sat on the wall by the wild flower garden, feeling surprisingly calm. This was where they'd met and this was where it would end. She breathed slowly, until her quiet tears finally came. She wept for the saddest of things; not just that Rolf was gone, but that he had died alone. No-one saw him go. No-one held his hand. No-one was able to say goodbye.

All through that day, Daisy wandered past the shed over and over again, unable to bring herself to go back inside. She watered the flowers, sat on the patio, pulled weeds out of the cracks in the path, sat on the patio, cut back some brambles, sat on the patio, picked some strawberries, sat on the patio, sat on the patio, sat on the patio.

Eventually, when the late sun began to set and the evening drew in, Daisy stood up and put her gloves and mask back on. She took her trowel, went to the farthest corner of the wild flower garden and dug a deep hole. She found a piece of soft white linen in her sewing cupboard, went into the shed, lifted Rolf gently from the doll's house bed and wrapped him up. She placed him in the hole and put the soil back.

"Goodbye, dear Rolf. I'm so glad I got to know you. You were a special friend."

She took two small pieces of cane stick and fashioned a cross, to mark his resting place, and planted a cutting of a cornflower on his grave. She closed her eyes and said a final, private goodbye to the friend who'd lived in her garden for ten years and who she'd only met in the last few weeks, when he knew she needed him the most. In a final act of practical cleanliness and emotional ritual, she made a small bonfire and burnt the doll's house bed and bedding. She could get new ones for Lois.

*

For the next few days, Daisy didn't feel like talking to anyone. She sent "I'm fine" emails if anyone asked about her, but didn't answer the phone when it rang. Instead, she sat in the garden, alone with her thoughts. The flowers, shrubs and trees no longer felt like companions. The garden felt empty, in spite of its blossom and foliage, because it was devoid of the fun and energy that had been Rolf.

Daisy decided to keep some of the routines that she'd followed with her little friend, and every evening, if it wasn't raining, she sat outside on the patio. One evening, when she was sitting there, admiring the bright full moon, Daisy jumped and tensed. A tiny shadow shape moved in the darkness at the end of the path. She knew it couldn't possibly be Rolf, although the shape looked to be about his height. It drew closer, walked slowly down the path, and took solid form. When it drew close enough, Daisy saw that it was a tiny little woman. She had Rolf's red hair, tied up in a bun, and was dressed in a long skirt and a jacket that were clearly cobbled together or hand-made, and which bore the dust and mud of time spent outdoors. The woman walked over to the edge of the patio, put her hands on her hips in a familiar stance and stared up at Daisy in the moonlight.

"Nancy," said Daisy.

"Yes."

"I'm Daisy."

"I just found him. Did you put him there? It's a nice spot. He always loved cornflowers the most. Thank you."

"It was the least I could do."

Nancy began to sob.

"What happened to him?"

Daisy explained the events of the teenage raid, and how the boys must have brought the virus into the garden.

"Did you know he was gone, before you got here?" Daisy asked.

"I felt it, here," Nancy beat furiously on her chest, "I lost his connection, his light, and so I had to come."

"I'm so sorry, Nancy. I only met Rolf a few weeks ago, but I want you to know that your brother was funny and kind," Daisy paused, "and brave."

"Can I sit up beside you?"

"Of course," said Daisy, and she lifted Nancy up onto the patio table.

"And he was so worried about you," Daisy continued. "I wanted to see if we could find a way to get out and see you. We did talk about it, but in the end we ran out of time."

"You did the right thing by staying here. We're all old," said Nancy.

"I miss him," said Daisy.

"So do I," Nancy turned to Daisy, "and if you don't mind, I'd like to stay around for a while, get to know Rolf's garden and be near him. My old lady went to stay with her family before the lockdown, so I don't think I'm going to be needed over in Maida Vale just yet."

"Of course. You can stay in the house with me, if you like."

"No, thank you. I'll stay in the garden. I like to keep my skills sharp."

Daisy laughed.

"That's what Rolf always said."

"Yes, we're definitely two of a kind."

The two women, one large and one very small, sat quietly together. They stared across the garden, taking in the moonlight view. Neither spoke for a while. There was no breeze, and the trees stood tall and still. The flowers slept. Daisy's beloved garden took on its most magical feel, and only Daisy and Nancy would ever feel it. Daisy would never be able to share this moment with anyone. After all, who would believe her?

Chapter 7

Harry's Story: 'One Good Turn'

The heavy snow had begun at first light, and the heaviness had kept the day dark. There was an eerie silence that only comes with snowfall and the thick snowflakes swirled and danced, quickly forming a deep white carpet. Harry had been trying for some time to clear a path to the garage so he could retrieve the car, but he had to accept that he was losing the battle. He was too old for this kind of work and no-one was there to help. Now his wintry foe was winning, and its attack couldn't have come at a worse time.

Harry leaned on his shovel, out of breath, and looked across the garden. The tree line boundary was a blurred image behind the snowy curtain and the road beyond was silent. Nobody was going anywhere today. Anyone with any sense was inside by the fire. Harry's boots sank into the snow as he pushed his way back to the house, where he leaned his shovel up against the wall and climbed the steps. He felt carefully for the wooden slats of the rickety front porch; now was not the time to fall and break something. Martha needed him.

Inside, Martha listened to the sound of boots stamping on the doormat, then the front door opened and closed again quietly.

"Harry?" she called.

Harry followed the sound of Martha's soft voice through to the living room. The fire he'd built earlier still crackled quietly in the hearth and Martha was still sitting exactly where he'd left her, on the edge of the bed by the window, dressed in her boots, coat and scarf, clutching her small overnight bag with both hands. He paused, then he went to hug her.

"I'm sorry, sweetheart," he whispered into her ear, "I can't get anywhere near the car."

"It's alright," she replied, turning to gaze up at him.

Slowly, she put down her bag and took off her coat. Harry pulled off her boots for her and helped her to sit back on the bed. He curled up beside her and they both stared out at the weather for a moment without speaking.

"Perhaps we can get there tomorrow," Martha said at last, "I'm sure it won't make that much difference if I don't get to the hospital today."

When Harry bent to kiss the top of her head, Martha missed the momentary look of pain that crossed his expression.

"I hope not," he whispered, and then cheered up, "Right, then. I'm going to make us both a nice cup of tea."

Martha didn't reply. She continued to watch out of the window. On his own in the kitchen, Harry gripped the countertop and closed his eyes. It had been really important that Martha got her treatment today, and they were trapped here.

When Harry carried their mugs of tea through, he was surprised to see that Martha had pulled herself up and was peering out into the garden. She was suddenly animated.

"Harry, come here, quickly!"

Harry put the drinks down on the windowsill and sat back down next to his wife.

"What is it?"

"Look," she whispered, "Over there."

He stared at the invading snow. It was falling faster than ever, and the evidence of his earlier efforts to cross the garden was already buried deep.

"What am I looking for?"

"Over there," Martha repeated, "There's something lying in the snow."

Harry squinted and tried to look through the blizzard.

"I can't see anything. All I can see is snowflakes."

"I'm sure I saw a buzzard fly at some little bird, and the poor thing fell out of the sky and landed in the garden. It was a little black shape. I can hardly see it now, but I know it's out there."

"Are you quite sure you saw something? Surely nothing's flying about in this weather," Harry ventured.

He put his arm around Martha and watched her. The doctors had warned him about this, that the illness tearing at Martha's brain might make his wife hallucinate, and he wasn't sure whether to believe her or not.

"Go and look, Harry. Maybe we can help."

Harry sighed.

"But I've only just come back inside. Can I drink my tea first?"

"Please. I don't think we should wait."

One of the things he'd always loved about his wife was her soft spot for rescuing things in distress. Over the years they'd helped all sorts of creatures, from tiny hedgehogs to majestic deer. Martha couldn't stand the idea that something was suffering, and now that she was suffering herself, Harry couldn't refuse.

"OK, I'll have a look."

He searched in the hallway for his spare coat and boots. A few minutes later he retraced his earlier journey back along the front porch and down the steps, and then he carefully walked around the edge of the house, leaning on its wooden walls for support, until he got to Martha's window. He looked upwards. Through the snow, he could make out her tiny face watching him, her expression both excited and anxious at the same time. He waved once and then turned to get his bearings.

The snow was deeper now and came up past Harry's knees. His progress was immediately laborious as he set off, following the direction Martha had indicated. The snow fell thick and fast, so that he had to wipe his face constantly to see through the melting flakes. His fingers and toes started to feel numb. Just as he was about to give up, go back and tell Martha that at least he'd tried, he saw the tip of a black feather protruding from the snow. He walked over and picked it up, then he saw another up ahead. Beside this second feather, several drops of red blood had blossomed through the snow, but there was no bird in sight. The poor thing had probably been buried by the blizzard already, but it might still be alive.

He knelt down next to the bloodstains, carefully scraped the snow away and let out a gasp of shock and surprise, because the first thing he found was not a beak or a beady eye, a wing or a claw. It was a hand, a perfectly-formed tiny hand. Quickly he scraped more snow away and uncovered a figure. Its delicate arms and legs were long and thin, and although it was no longer than his forearm, the figure was a perfect miniature of a young woman. She was dressed in a shift of coarse cloth and her sleek black hair spread around her. Her face was pointed and pale, and her eyes were closed.

Harry assumed the tiny thing was just a doll, but why it would be lying in their garden was beyond him. There were no neighbours for miles around. He leaned forward and put his hands underneath her to ease her out, and he stopped dead. When he lifted her, she definitely wasn't a doll, all plastic and stiff. She was malleable and soft. Her body bent as he moved her. Then, when he laid her across his arm and turned her over to examine her, he discovered the source of the feathers. Two delicate wings protruded from her shoulders. One of them was bent a little out of place, and dried blood had congealed around the veins at its joint. As Harry watched her, fascinated, she stirred a little and let out a sigh. He almost dropped her in fright when he realised she was alive.

"Oh, my," Harry said out loud, "What's Martha going to say when she sees you?"

He made his way back to the house, his arms wrapped around his sleeping charge. He didn't stop to take off his coat and boots. He walked straight through to where Martha was waiting and placed the tiny woman on her lap.

"Oh, my goodness! Look what you found! It's a fairy! Is she real?"

"She's real, alright. Isn't she just beautiful?"

"Oh, Harry, ever since we were children, there were stories about the fairy folk in these woods, but I thought that's all they were – stories."

"Well, she's here with us now. She just looks like she's fast asleep, doesn't she, but be careful there, Martha. Look, her wing's hurt."

"Poor thing. What should we do, Harry?"

"I've no idea. Can't take her any place anyway in this weather."

"Why don't you lie her down in front of the fire? Here, take one of my pillows."

"OK. Give her here."

Harry gently lifted the fairy from Martha's lap and carried her over to the fire, where he laid her down on her side to keep from crushing her damaged wing. He tucked Martha's pillow under her head, and she stayed that way all afternoon, sleeping soundly, Harry and Martha keeping an eye on her, while the snow continued to fall, keeping the three of them inside.

That evening Martha slept soundly in her bed by the window. Harry was relieved that she'd coped with the day's events so well. In front of the fire, the tiny fairy also slept soundly.

Harry took the opportunity to go through to the kitchen and watch some television. He'd taken one of the armchairs and the television through there some time ago, so he could watch something without disturbing Martha, when she got so tired she couldn't climb the stairs anymore. Miraculously, the television still had reception despite the snow. Harry poured himself a whiskey and settled down to watch a quiz show. Later there'd be a movie or highlights of a football game. Meanwhile, the blizzard still blew outside, and now and then the whistling wind was caught in the chimney and hummed in a weird sing-song voice.

Harry felt himself dozing off before the quiz show was half-way through. He was just closing his eyes, allowing himself the luxury of a nap while Martha didn't need anything, when he was disturbed by the creak of a floorboard next door. He sat up, alert immediately, and listened. A second creak told Harry that someone of weight – not his sick wife or a tiny fairy – was moving around next door.

Harry crept across to the cutlery drawer and took out a sharp knife. He knew this house well. He knew every nook and cranny, every gap in the wooden walls, the feel of every individual draught. He'd been born and raised here, brought Martha here and raised their son here, expected to die here, and this was why he knew which creaking floorboards to avoid himself as he headed towards the living room door. When he reached it, he stood and listened to quiet shuffling sounds on the other side. He opened the door just a tiny crack, jumped in fright and almost dropped the knife.

A man was standing in the shadows by the fireplace. As Harry watched, he bent down and gently reached his hand towards the sleeping fairy. Mindful of the safety of both his wife and their sleeping guest, and full of Dutch courage brought on by the whiskey, Harry stepped into the room, knife pointed in a shaking hand, and crept up behind the stranger.

"Don't. Move," he whispered.

Unexpectedly, the man did as he was told without any protest, and Harry got a good look at him. He was young. His long black hair fell to his shoulders and he was wrapped in a dark cloak. He looked tall and strong. Harry weighed up the situation and knew he would be no match for him in a struggle, until he noticed the deformity hidden below the man's cloak. The young man, handsome enough, appeared to be sadly blighted by a humped back.

"Can I stand up, please?" the man whispered.

Harry kept the knife pointed at him.

"Alright, but move slowly."

The man stood up and turned towards Harry. He was much taller than Harry had first anticipated and he looked down at Harry with strange, piercing blue eyes which gleamed in the firelight.

"Who are you?" Harry whispered.

"My name is Enzo. May I ask your name?"

"I'm Harry Smith. This is my home, mine and Martha's. How did you get in here?"

"If I told you," Enzo replied, "you wouldn't believe me."

"What do you want? We haven't got any money."

"You have nothing to fear from me. I mean you no harm."

"Then why are you here?"

"I just came to get my wife."

He indicated to the sleeping fairy.

"Your wife?" said Harry, incredulous.

"Yes. Her name is Rafka."

"How can she be your wife? You're human, and she's tiny."

"Don't be deceived by appearances, Harry. I'm not human, and Rafka is not tiny."

Enzo made a move to put his hand under his cloak.

"Stop!" said Harry, "I said, don't move."

Enzo spread his hands wide in submission.

"I only wanted to show you something, to prove a point."

"And I told you to keep still."

"Very well, but at least let me explain."

"About what?"

"I was only trying to take off my cloak, to show you that I have wings too."

There was a moment of silence while Harry considered this.

"Alright," he indicated a 'go ahead' with his knife, "Show me."

Enzo unfastened his cloak and dropped it to the floor. Slowly he turned around, and Harry saw that he did not have a deformity after all, but a pair of large wings. They shone sleek and black in the firelight and looked exactly the same as those of the sleeping fairy.

"Oh, my," Harry whispered. He could think of nothing else to say.

"Can I sit down?" asked Enzo.

Harry nodded. Enzo sat down in an armchair, his wings folded behind him, and Harry, relaxing a little, sank onto the edge of Martha's bed. He glanced at her. She was fast asleep.

"Where did you find Rafka?" Enzo continued.

"In the garden, this afternoon. My wife thought she saw a buzzard attack something and it fell out of the sky. We thought it was a little bird."

A flash of concern passed over Enzo's face.

"Thank you for taking care of her. I warned her not to go flying in this storm, but she so loves to fly through the snow. It doesn't usually snow this heavily and she wanted to get out and have some fun. I lost her for a while and then I sensed that she was here. She led me to your house."

"What do you mean?"

"We fairies can sense each other, our feelings, our needs, our whereabouts and so on, but now that I know she was hurt, that explains why her senses became weak and I lost track of her."

"We weren't sure what to do. We thought it best to keep her warm by the fire," said Harry.

"Which really helped, and she's been able to get enough strength back to lead me here."

Harry looked across at the sleeping fairy.

"I know what you're thinking," Enzo commented. "You're still wondering how she's so small and I'm not?"

Harry shrugged his shoulders.

"Fairies are not small creatures," said Enzo, "We're more like humans in size, but the difference between us is, we can change and become very small. The only time we do this is when we need a lot of energy. Rafka became small to be able to fly fast in the snow."

"And that's how the buzzard was able to attack her."

"Yes. But, being small also enables us to conserve our energy and use it to survive. That's why Rafka is staying small while she's asleep. She's been waiting for me to get here."

Harry paused.

"This is a lot to take in," he said, "I mean, I can see you both have wings and all, but are you really fairies?"

Enzo smiled.

"I can't make you believe me, Harry, but what else can you trust better than your own eyes? Now, could I trouble you for a spoon, the smallest spoon you have? I want to give Rafka some drops of this medicine."

He put his hand into his pocket and pulled out a small glass bottle. The glass was clear, and Harry could see an amber liquid inside. He wondered what it might be.

"We have teaspoons in the kitchen," he replied, "but I think perhaps they'd be too big?"

"I can try."

Harry paused.

"Oh, wait. I have some pipettes. You know what they are? Martha..."

Harry indicated to his own sleeping wife.

"My wife, Martha, she's very sick. She gets really weak sometimes after her chemo and I use a pipette to give her some of her medicine. Wait here and I'll get one."

"Thank you."

In the kitchen, Harry opened the box of medical supplies the hospital had given him and took out a new pipette, still in a sealed sterile wrapper. When he went back through to the living room, he found Enzo sitting on the floor next to Rafka, stroking her hair and talking gently. He didn't notice Harry come in, and for a moment Harry stood quietly, listening to Enzo speaking in a strange language. Harry couldn't understand it at all, but it sounded beautiful, so ancient and pure.

"Hmmm," Harry eventually cleared his throat, "Here you are."

He tore open the sterile wrapping and showed Enzo how to draw some of the amber liquid up into the pipette. Enzo lifted Rafka onto his lap, held her head back and gently pushed her mouth open with his finger. He squeezed the pipette into her mouth and closed it again, then he lay her back down and tended to her damaged wing, manoeuvring it gently and rubbing some more of the amber liquid around its injured joint. Now and then he spoke to her in gentle hushed tones, and Harry was moved by Enzo's obvious love and care.

"Thank you, Harry," Enzo said, as he stood up, "Now we just have to wait."

"Would you like some tea?" Harry asked, "I mean, do you drink tea?"

"I can try it," Enzo replied, smiling, "Thank you."

A few minutes later, they sat in silence with their drinks, watching the two sleeping women.

"I know Rafka will get better," Enzo whispered, suddenly turning to Harry, "and quickly, but is Martha going to get better?"

"I don't know. I just don't know. She's very sick. She has cancer. Do you know what that is? It frightens me, the thought of losing her. I feel so helpless."

Harry got up, walked across to the window and stared at the night sky. With everything that had been going on in the house, he hadn't noticed that the snow had finally stopped, and now the moonlight shone over a brilliant, shining landscape, smooth, silent and still. It's not fair, he thought. Why can't *I* have some magic to heal *my* wife? He swallowed before he continued.

"I was supposed to get Martha to the hospital today for her next treatment, but I can't clear a way out of here by myself, and my son can't get here to help me. The news reports said the roads are all closed. We'll get there as soon as we can, but I'm scared it'll set her back a bit."

Just then, Martha stirred a little and lifted her head. Harry turned away from the window to look at her.

"Hey there," she whispered, smiling, "How's our little fairy doing?"

"Well," Harry replied, "A lot's been happening while you've been asleep."

Harry was about to explain what he meant when he noticed that Martha was staring towards the fireplace, a surprised expression on her face. He turned to look.

Rafka was awake. She was no longer small. She stood tall and proud next to Enzo, who held a protective arm around her as she leaned into him. They were both smiling.

"Hello, Martha," said Enzo, "I'm Enzo and this is my wife, Rafka. Thanks to you and Harry, she's going to be alright."

"Thank you for helping me," said Rafka. When she spoke, her voice tinkled across the quiet room.

"But you were so small," Martha whispered, in awe.

"Because I was hurt. I went flying in the blizzard – oh, how I love flying in the snow – but I didn't expect that bird to attack me. It caught my wing in its claws but I struggled and managed to break free. The last thing I remember is falling out of control and hitting the snow."

"I saw you!" Martha called out excitedly. "I saw you fall. I told Harry, but he thought I was imagining it."

"Well, I just thought..." Harry began, a little embarrassed.

"No matter," said Rafka, "I'm so glad you saw me, Martha, and that Harry was able to find me. You saved me. My wing was only dislocated. Enzo was able to re-set it. See?"

She stood up, turned around and spread both wings out. Their majestic symmetry filled the room.

"Oh!" Martha whispered, as she stared at the delicate cobweb patterns which flashed across Rafka's wings. "They're beautiful!"

"Neat, huh!" Rafka said, in mock human-speak and they all laughed.

"Harry," said Martha, turning to her husband, "we should make our visitors something to eat."

Now it was Enzo who spoke.

"Really, there's no need, Martha." He leaned forward and took her hand in his, "And also, there's no time."

Martha looked up at the fairy man.

"Why not?"

"You and Harry did us a good turn. We want to repay your kindness, and we can do that right now."

"You don't need to repay anything," Harry replied, "We're glad we could help."

"Yes," Martha agreed, "And it was all meant to be. If we'd got the car out and gone to the hospital, I wouldn't have seen you fall and told Harry to go and find you, so it's funny how things work out."

Enzo turned to Harry.

"It's important that Martha gets to the hospital."

"Yes, very."

"Well, we can take you there."

Harry thought of the television weather reports about the snow-blocked roads. He looked at the fairy couple. They were both smiling a 'knowing' smile at him, as if they knew something Harry didn't.

"But how?" he asked.

"We'll fly, of course."

"What – you mean carry us, up there in the sky?"

Enzo looked serious now.

"You have no idea how strong we fairies are. We can easily carry you."

Harry looked at Martha, pondering on this incredible offer. Martha smiled.

"Let's do it," she whispered.

Harry went to the hallway and collected Martha's winter coat, hat, scarf, gloves and fur-lined boots, while Enzo and Rafka carefully helped her out of bed. Beside the two strong, healthy fairy people, his wife looked minute and frail. Harry felt a lump in his throat and pushed away tears.

"Come on, dear. Gotta wrap you up tight," he called.

Martha pushed her arms into the waiting coat sleeves.

"Is it cold in the sky?" she asked.

"We don't think so," Rafka replied, "but you might, so wrap up well."

Harry was terrified and hoped it didn't show. Was he doing the right thing, trusting these people? What if, somehow, they weren't fairies and this is a sham? What if they were real, but not as strong as they thought? What if they fell while they were carrying them? What if they…? What if? What if? What if?

Harry knew deep down they had no choice but to do this. They might be stuck here for days or even weeks if the snow continued. Choking back tears, he helped Martha to fasten her coat up tight and wrap her scarf around her neck. She pulled on her woollen hat and gloves, then held onto Enzo while she stepped into her boots. Harry quickly pulled on his own warm clothing.

"I'll just get your overnight bag, Martha."

"And then we're ready to go!" she said cheerfully.

Enzo and Rafka helped Martha towards the front door. They gently held her elbows and supported her slow progress, while Harry followed behind, carrying her bag. Out on the front porch, it was silent. The crisp, undisturbed snow glinted and sparkled and the air smelt fresh and clear.

"What a beautiful evening," Rafka commented, then she turned to the couple, "I'll take Martha, and Enzo will take you, Harry."

Harry nodded anxiously. He watched Rafka as she bent down and easily picked up his wife, one arm under her knees and another around her waist. Martha put an arm around Rafka's neck. When she looked across at Harry, her eyes were glinting with excitement.

"This is going to be fun, Harry!" she announced.

Rafka carried Martha down the porch steps and into an open space in the garden. As she walked across the deep snow, she didn't sink into it the way Harry had earlier, and he wondered how she managed to do that. More magic? Was she light as a feather despite her size? Harry had no time to keep wondering, because now Rafka tensed and shuddered a little, as if in anticipation. She spread out her wings. There was a brief pause. Rafka looked back once at Enzo and Harry over her shoulder, smiled at them and then suddenly shot up into the air.

"Oh my," Harry whispered for the second time that evening, as his wife disappeared into the dark sky, growing smaller and smaller as they flew upwards. Rafka flapped her wings vigorously and when she reached a particular height, she slowed this movement to a glide, leaned gently in a circular move to the left and began to fly forwards, heading west towards town.

"Don't you worry, Harry. We'll soon catch them," Enzo said. "Come on."

As he bent down and lifted Harry up, in the same way Rafka had lifted Martha, Harry wondered if they both carried humans about on a regular basis. He held on as Enzo opened his wings, paused for just a moment, in which Harry felt that funny little pull you get just before a plane takes off, and then whoosh! They flew up into the sky and chased after their two wives.

Enzo soon caught up to Rafka but stayed a little bit behind her. The two fairies flew in silence. Harry could feel the gentle coming and going of their wings, the subtle changes in angle as they turned, and the rhythm made him feel curiously safe. Below them, the white world stretched as far as the eye could see. The roads were deserted. Only now and then did an occasional beam of headlights snake and wind as some vehicle struggled along. The snow had brought the world to a standstill, and Harry was full of gratitude that they'd met their strange new friends.

In what seemed no time at all, the hospital buildings loomed into view below. The light from its many windows sent streaks across the snow, and now and then blue lights could be seen moving about. The two fairies slowly began to descend, and as they got closer, Harry could make out the people who, like a colony of ants, were hurrying about between the buildings.

The huge car park at the rear of the hospital had been cleared of snow, but it was still deserted. Rafka made her way towards the darkest corner. Her descent to earth became slower and slower, until she was almost hovering, then she put her feet down and walked to a controlled halt. Enzo followed seconds later and landed in the same way. As the fairies gently helped Martha and Harry to stand on the cleared ground, Martha couldn't contain her excitement.

"Oh Harry! That's the most wonderful thing I ever did!"

"Wasn't it just!" Rafka laughed. "Come on, let's get you inside."

The two fairies led the old couple across the car park, to where a covered walkway led into the hospital's main reception. It was lit by low-level ceiling lights, dry and snow free.

"Well, we know the way from here," said Harry.

He looked at Enzo and Rafka. Their wings were folded behind them and they stood together, holding hands, their pale skin shining in the artificial light.

"I can never thank you enough," he said.

"And neither can I," Martha added.

"You helped me," Rafka replied, "and now we have helped you."

There was an awkward silence.

"Will we ever see you again?" said Martha, voicing Harry's thoughts.

"We tend to keep ourselves hidden," Rafka replied, "living alongside you without you knowing we're there. Humans are not always as kind to us as you have been, and so it would be nice to think we can meet again."

"So, will you come and see us? Can you find our house again?" Harry asked now.

"Of course," Rafka continued. "We would never forget, but now you must go inside. Goodbye, until we meet again."

Rafka stepped forwards and hugged first Martha, then Harry. Enzo put his hand on Harry's shoulder and quietly slipped something into his coat pocket.

"You can trust in this," he whispered, "I promise it will work."

He stepped away again.

"Good luck, both of you," he called, "and goodbye."

Enzo led his wife away into the darkness of the car park. They both turned back once to wave and then they shook open their wings and shot away together into the sky. Harry and Martha watched them go until they disappeared completely among the stars, then they set off along the walkway.

"Are we dreaming, Harry?" asked Martha.

"No, dear, we're not."

"You know, I have an especially good feeling about my treatment. There's something magic in the air."

"Yes," Harry agreed, and he put his hand in his pocket and felt the familiar little bottle of amber liquid.

At the entrance to the oncology ward, the night sister hurried to greet them.

"You got here. Thank goodness. What weather! You didn't drive, did you?"

"No," said Harry. "Lucky for us, we were able to get a lift from some friends."

Chapter 8

Bill's Story: '444 – For Fun, For Fear, For Friendship'

Bill stood in the care home lobby, turning his head every time someone came through the double front doors. He leaned against the reception desk, gnarled fingers clutching the rounded corner of the counter. He was a little unsteady on his feet, but his mind was sharp, his jaw was set rigid and his eyes, hawk-like, darted everywhere.

Behind him, clinking cups and saucers and distant voices emanated from the day room, where some of the other residents were meeting their visitors. Some had no visitors at all, and occupied themselves alone or sat complacently staring into space.

"I'm waiting for my grandson, you know," Bill told the receptionist, who smiled because he'd told her about fifty times already. "He's been in Australia for two years, doing the Big Travel."

He'd already told her that too, but the receptionist didn't mind. She was fond of Bill. He was different. He liked to flash his tattoos at the lady residents when he was feeling mischievous. He was the only old biker in the home and he dressed like one. His silver-grey hair was always pulled back in a ponytail, he insisted on wearing oily jeans and his bony elbows stuck out of T-shirts on which were displayed famous racing teams and meetings from the motorbike world.

"Hey, Grandad! Here I am!" called a voice.

Bill turned and smiled. A young man, tall and tanned, dressed in jeans and a motorbike jacket, bounced through the front door and across the lobby. He towered over his grandfather and leaned down to kiss the top of his head.

"Hi, Grandad."

"Michael, just look at you! You look so well!"

"Of course. That's what the Aussie sun, sand and surf does for you!"

"Should we get some tea?" said Bill, pointing. "Look, the trolley's just coming."

"I wouldn't mind a cup of tea," said Michael, "but let's go somewhere else, eh?"

"What've you got in mind?"

Michael winked.

"Come on. I've got a surprise."

Outside in the car park, Michael gently held Bill's elbow to guide him down the steps and past the row of visitor's cars. When they reached the end and they were standing by the gate, Bill let out a gasp of surprise. Parked in front of him, in all its glory, was a vintage motorbike, complete with sidecar. Bill looked longingly at the polished headlight, the silver petrol tank, the shining girder suspension forks, the smart leather saddle. The afternoon sun glinted off the chrome handlebars and levers.

"My old Norton!" Bill croaked hoarsely, his voice overcome as he shuffled over and stroked the handlebars. "Last time I saw her, she was underneath a dust sheet in your Dad's garage. God, if only I were ten years younger, I'm sure I could still manage to handle her."

"Dad and Uncle Jim have been working on her in secret while I was away. They put the sidecar on and now," Michael bowed towards the motorbike and spread his hands in a welcoming gesture, "you and I are going for a homecoming spin."

He walked across to the sidecar and pulled out a motorcycle jacket.

"And my old Belstaff. Your Dad kept it!!" Bill declared, as he let Michael help him to ease each arm into the sleeves and then fasten all the zips and buckles. He closed his eyes and smelt the familiar saddle wax and old engine oil.

"And here's your gloves and scarf as well, but I'm afraid I didn't bring your helmet and goggles. They belong in a museum! I brought you my spare helmet."

Michael helped his grandfather step into the sidecar, where he wriggled around in the seat.

"See? You might be too old to ride the bike, but you're never too old to be a passenger, eh?"

Next Michael eased his helmet over his grandfather's head, pulled the visor down and checked the strap under his chin, before he pulled on his own helmet and swung his leg over the saddle. He jumped down hard on the kick start. The engine turned over first time. When he turned the throttle a few times, the initial low throaty growl changed to a menacing bellow. The rhythm of the engine seemed to pass through the two of them and down into the earth. Michael gave Bill a thumbs-up. Bill responded by patting him enthusiastically on the leg and pointing forwards.

"Alright, alright." Michael laughed. "Let's go!"

They pulled out of the car park and set off down the road. Bill clutched the front of the sidecar with both hands, adrenaline rushing through him and the wind whipping past. He closed his eyes, listened to the engine and felt the G-force press against him as the Norton navigated every corner of the twisting lanes. He was one with the motorbike as it went faster or slowed down, responding to every touch of the throttle and brake as if he were riding it himself. Memories of his days on the road tumbled over themselves. He was in Heaven!

As they rounded the next bend, they slowed down to approach a T-junction on the right hand side. Bill opened his eyes just in time to see an old Triumph motorbike pull out of the junction, its rider anonymous behind his helmet and goggles. The growl of the Norton was joined by the roar of the Triumph as it set off in front of them. Bill watched it lean into each corner ahead of them, and he hoped Michael would rise to the challenge of keeping up with it if it sped away. They followed the Triumph in this way for a couple of miles, through left turns and right turns, the sharper the better, the unspoken camaraderie of the two-wheeled traveller driving them on.

Suddenly the Triumph rider braked. Michael caught up and was only a few yards from his tail light. That's when Bill noticed the licence plate. He looked at it, blinked in shock and looked again. He clutched the sidecar even tighter and watched the Triumph as it sped away.

"Faster, Michael! Go on! Catch him up!" he shouted, but Michael didn't seem to hear him.

"Damn these full-face helmets," he muttered to himself. He tapped Michael's thigh with a bony forefinger and pointed ahead. "Hurry, hurry," he was trying to say. Michael looked down quickly at his grandfather's gesticulations, sensed he wanted to play, and opened up the throttle again. This time the Triumph seemed to slow down deliberately, waiting for them, and they soon caught up again.

Bill stared at the license plate, certain this time that his old eyes weren't tricking him. There it was. EVB 444. There was no doubt in Bill's mind. Their old motto: '444, for fun, for fear, for friendship,' had been coined from this very licence plate. This wasn't just any old Triumph. It was Jackie's bike.

Tears sprang into Bill's eyes. How could Jackie's bike be on the road? Who's got it, and how? That bike was long-wrecked, irretrievable. He was there. He saw it. Bill stared ahead at the tail light as Michael accelerated and slowed, now keeping up and then letting the Triumph get away. Bill thought back to a dark July night. They'd been on a late-night run, just the two of them. On the way home, there'd been a sudden tight bend, a slippery road, a tree on the corner. Just like now, the Triumph had been racing ahead of his Norton, which was trusty but not as quick. For a split second,

Jackie had rounded the corner and was out of sight. There was a sound of impact, of splintering whining metal, and when Bill rounded the corner seconds later he was already too late. That was the last time he saw his friend, all those years ago, more than sixty years ago, on a night that Bill had always wanted to remember and wanted to forget at the same time. He took a deep breath and asked himself again: Who's got the bike now?

Suddenly the Triumph slowed rapidly and stopped on the side of the lane. Michael roared past and Bill, caught unawares, had no time to look at the other rider. He tried to turn around in his seat but his old bones wouldn't let him. For a moment his stomach churned and then, with relief, he heard the sound of the Triumph engine pulling up behind. He tried to turn round again but to no avail. Who's behind us? Who's got Jackie's bike?

The Triumph followed behind for a while. Bill could hear the two engines singing in harmony, they were that close. He leaned a little to see if he could catch the bike in Michael's mirror, but he was too low down. Unable to turn around, he cursed at his aged bones as he sensed the Triumph had come up even closer. Why? Why didn't the rider overtake? They travelled for some time in this way, twisting and turning. Bill clutched the sidecar, staring ahead, a sense of irritation and helplessness spoiling his ride.

Suddenly, the Triumph overtook them and was back in front again, and once again, everything happened so fast that Bill didn't get to see the rider. He heard a beep-beep on the Triumph's horn for the few seconds they were level, saw a flash of goggles, of gloves clutching the handle bars, of someone in a soft leather helmet, and then the bike was past. Bill felt a wave of panic and frustration; twice he'd missed getting a good look at the rider.

The two machines travelled on in sync, the one leading, the other following, and Bill felt better when he could see the other bike in front. Perhaps it would be nice to give a wave. The rider in front would see him in his mirror. He lifted his right hand cautiously and when he signalled to the Triumph, he instinctively used the old signal, an agreed sign; a thumbs up followed by a clenched fist and then another thumbs up. To his surprise, and shock, the rider turned in his seat and signalled back to Bill in exactly the same way.

Suddenly, although he couldn't understand how, Bill knew for sure who was riding his friend's motorbike. His breathing slowed down. He relaxed back into the sidecar seat. He held less fiercely onto the sides, and inside Michael's full-face helmet, he smiled to himself. The Triumph rode on for a while and then turned without warning into a left hand junction. Bill tried to look down the lane as Michael sped past. He just got a glimpse of the Triumph disappearing round another bend.

"No, no! Michael! Stop! We have to go back!" he shouted, but it was no use. Michael carried on oblivious, and Bill's words were lost amid the wind and the engine roar.

Eventually Michael slowed down, indicated and turned into the car park of a pretty country pub, a stone building covered in ivy and clematis. He parked up, turned off the engine, jumped off the bike and went round to help his grandfather out of his seat. Bill made no move to get out. He sat very still. Michael leaned over, undid the strap of Bill's helmet and gently lifted it off. Bill blinked in the sunlight but continued to sit still.

"Grandad – are you alright?"

Michael waited. His grandfather was miles away, deep in thought. Eventually he turned to his grandson.

"Sorry. I was just thinking about old times."

Michael smiled.

"Come on. Let me help you out."

They decided to sit outside at a picnic table, underneath a large parasol, where a waitress brought them tea and scones.

"So," Michael asked, "Did you enjoy the ride here?"

"Oh, it was amazing! I love my old Norton. She's like a second missus."

"And that old Triumph was a beauty, eh? We had a bit of a cat-and-mouse going on, and there was a moment when he got right up behind us. It was almost as if he was having a look at us. Did you notice?"

"Yes," said Bill, "I did."

"And he seemed quite young too. People my age usually go for the speed and the power. You know, they want to pretend they're Valentino Rossi or Mark Marquez and they're on a race track. It's thanks to you I'm hooked on the old timers."

"Well," replied Bill, "that Triumph rider is never going to feel old like me and have my aches and pains. He'll never be told he's too old to ride any more and have to be driven around in a sidecar by his grandson."

"How do you know that?"

Bill smiled.

"Oh, trust me, I just know."

<u>Chapter 9</u>

**<u>Emma's Story: 'Look Who Came to Help
When You Were On Your Own'</u>**

Fingers of lightning flashed through Emma's bedroom curtains. She lay curled up on her side, listening as the thunder claps came closer and closer, counting the seconds in between just like she did when she was a child. She nursed a headache which seemed to pound more and more in time with the storm. Finally she could bear it no longer. She sat up, swung her legs over the side of the bed and got up in search of painkillers.

She peeped into Katie's room, and then into Jake's. They were both fast asleep, undisturbed, arms flung wide, deep in their dreams. As she turned to leave Jake's room she noticed that the window was open a little. The curtains blew gently in the breeze. For certain it was closed when she had tucked Jake into bed. She walked across to the window and pulled it shut, making a mental note to remind him not to open it again when he settled down for the night.

Back in the hallway, Emma stopped by the telephone table at the top of the stairs and flicked the light switch. Nothing happened. Power's down. She stepped carefully onto the dark stairs and held onto the banister. Step by careful step, she went down the stairs, her journey lit up now and then when the lightning flashed through the windows. Just as she was almost at the bottom she missed her footing, slipped awkwardly and fell backwards. She lay there for a moment, winded, and rubbed at a strange pointed pain in her left side.

In the kitchen she found some paracetamol in a drawer and poured a glass of water. She swallowed the tablets, put the glass back on the drainer and turned to go back to bed. Suddenly a particularly bright flash of lightning lit up the kitchen and Emma stopped in her tracks, because she was sure she saw someone.

When her eyes recovered from the lightning flash, she looked again and saw an old woman in a dressing gown and slippers, her hair tied up in a bun, standing in the corner by the back door. For a moment the two women stared at each other, then

Emma's breathing slowed and she regained her composure.

"Who are you? What are you doing?" Emma challenged, "And how did you get in? Did you break in?"

"This is *my* house. Why would I break into my own house?"

The old woman stepped forwards as she spoke.

"I woke up just now with a terrible headache and came down to find some paracetamol, but I'm confused. The kitchen looks just like it did years ago, before we renovated it."

"Listen," said Emma patiently, "this is my house, not yours. I don't know how you got in here, but you need to go home. Where do you live? Is there someone I can call?"

The old woman shuffled across to the kitchen table, sat down and stared at Emma. She stared for a long time before she spoke.

"I know you," she said quietly.

"You do?"

"Yes. You're Emma Phillips."

"What? How do you know my name?"

"You have two small children, Jake and Katie. Your husband is called Paul. He works away a lot."

Emma slowly crossed the kitchen and sat down opposite the old woman.

"Are you staying with one of our neighbours? Did they tell you about me?"

"You work in the library. You always finish at two-thirty so you can collect the children from school. Recently, there was a terrible snow storm. The car wouldn't start. You had to get the bus. You tried to get a message to school but no-one answered the phone. It was the first time you'd ever been late and the children were upset because..."

"Because they thought I'd had an accident. How do you know these things about us?"

The old woman didn't reply, but pressed on.

"Your birthday is April fifteenth."

"That's right."

"How old will you be next birthday?"

"Thirty-five."

"Then the year is 1976."

"Yes, of course it is, but listen. Stop talking about me. Who are you?"

The old woman paused for a moment. She looked directly at Emma before she spoke.

"I'm Emma Phillips," she replied. "I'll be sixty-five on April fifteenth. My children, Jake and Katie, are grown up and I'm a grandma now. The year is 2006."

For a moment Emma stared at the old woman, lost for words. The thunder rumbled in the background to their silence.

"You think we're the same person? But that's not possible!"

"Maybe, but if you were with me in 2006, instead of me being here, I could show you photos of what I looked like, thirty years ago. I recognised you straight away."

"You're telling me that you've travelled back in time? Don't be ridiculous!"

The old woman looked around the kitchen. She seemed to be considering something.

"What's the date?"

"January fourteenth. Why?"

Emma watched as the old woman suddenly closed her eyes and shuddered. When she opened her eyes again she looked grim.

"Paul is away on business," she whispered.

"Yes. He'll be back tomorrow."

"You and the children are alone here."

"Stop it. You're scaring me."

"Listen to me. You'll be alright but you have to be strong."

"Why do I need to be strong?"

"Because something's happening."

"What are you talking about? Nothing's happening. We're just sitting here talking."

"And now we can't talk anymore."

"Why not?"

"Because you have to get up."

The old woman pushed her chair back and stood up.

"Get up, Emma," she said firmly.

Emma stared up at the old woman's face, confused.

"Why? What's the matter?"

The old woman's expression became more urgent.

"I said get up!"

Still Emma didn't move. She watched the old woman brace herself and take a deep breath.

"Get up!" she screamed at Emma. "Right now!"

Emma responded this time and stood up quickly. Immediately she was struck by a vicious pain in her left side which made her legs crumple beneath her. She fell to the floor. When she tried to stand up again the room started to sway. She reached to lean on the kitchen table and pull herself up, but the hard-edged corner of the table was gone. Emma felt instead the smooth polished wood of the banister in the hallway, because she was no longer in the kitchen. She was lying at the bottom of the stairs, on her back, exactly where she'd tripped and fallen earlier. The old woman was standing over her. Emma looked around the hallway, confused.

"Listen to me," the old woman whispered. "Someone is in the house.

They've hurt you but you're going to be alright."

Only now did Emma become aware of a stickiness on her nightdress. She looked down at a red stain which was seeping through the cotton fabric. Blood was trickling down her thigh, over her knee and onto the carpet.

"What's happened to me?" she shouted, horrified.

The old woman put her finger to her lips and gestured a 'Sssssh'.

"You've been stabbed," she whispered.

"Help me!"

"Come on. We have to use the upstairs phone. We can't get to the other one. Someone's in the front room."

Emma struggled to her feet and wrapped her left arm around the old woman's shoulder. She pressed her right hand over her wound, trying to stem the flow of blood, and together the two women struggled up the stairs, step by synchronised step. When they finally reached the phone on the landing, Emma leaned against the wall, breathing heavily, her blood-soaked nightdress sticking to her skin.

"I'm going to die," she whispered.

"No, you're not. I can tell you that for sure. Now, pick up the phone."

Emma dialled 999. A man's voice answered on the first ring.

"Which service do you require?"

"The police, and an ambulance."

"Who's hurt?"

"Me. I've been stabbed, by an intruder."

"What's your name?"

"Emma. Emma Phillips."

"Keep calm, Emma. Just breathe slowly. Now, what's your address?"

"Seventeen, The Cedars, Collerton Square."

"The police and paramedics are on their way. Is anyone else in the house?"

"My children are asleep in their rooms. Emma is here next to me."

"Emma? But you said you're Emma, right?"

"Yes. I'm young Emma and I think she's old Emma."

"I'm sorry, you're not making sense."

Emma was about to reply when a man in dark clothing suddenly walked through from the front room. He stood at the bottom of the stairs, his eyes staring up at Emma menacingly from behind a black ski mask. Emma saw the bloodied knife in his hand and could only watch, petrified, as he began to walk up the stairs. The old woman held Emma's hand tightly.

"Stay calm. He's going to leave," she whispered through clenched teeth, "Just ..about.. now."

At that moment the sound of distant sirens interrupted the tension. The intruder turned his head in the direction of the sound, listening. He paused on the third stair. He looked at Emma once more, then turned and ran quickly into the kitchen. Emma heard him pull back the bolts on the kitchen door, turn the key and open the door. She let go of the old woman's hand and eased herself carefully down onto the floor. Blue lights flashed through the windows at the front of the house, followed by the sound of breaking glass as the police broke through the front door. Emma heard voices calling her name. The old woman leaned forward and gently touched Emma's shoulder.

"I'm going," she whispered. "You'll be safe now."

"But where are you going?"

The old woman smiled.

"Back to bed, of course. My headache's quite gone."

"You saved me," she whispered.

"Oh, no," the old woman replied. "You made the phone call. You just saved me."

Emma watched the old woman shuffle away along the landing, just as the police and paramedics hurried towards her up the stairs. A policeman went to check on the children, while a paramedic talked soothingly, examined Emma's wound and inserted a drip in her arm. As Emma was lifted onto a stretcher, she looked along the hallway, just in time to see the old woman disappear through her own bedroom door.

Chapter 10

George's Story: 'Making Plans'

The estate agent unlocked the front door and stepped back to let Laura enter first. He smiled that knowing smile which he kept for the clients he thought would be a pushover. Inside, Laura glanced around the open plan living area.

"As you can see, it's a simple affair and comes unfurnished, but that's reflected in the price," he began his spiel. "The galley kitchen is over here. The bedroom is through on the right..."

"Where's the bathroom?" Laura asked curtly.

"Er, this way."

Laura took a long time to inspect the bathroom, the estate agent thought, considering she seemed totally disinterested in the rest of the apartment. Weird, but who cares as long as she wants to rent.

"I'll take it," Laura said, "for two months."

"The usual rental period is six."

Laura looked at the estate agent, weighed him up; social climber in a fancy suit.

"And your point is?" she challenged.

The young man crumbled under the weight of the older woman's gaze.

"Nothing," he said. "Two months is fine."

"Good. I'll call by the office to sign the lease."

*

When Laura visited her secret apartment for the last time, she followed the same routine she'd used on the first, second, third and every subsequent visit. She left her carrier bag in the bathroom and carried on through to the still-empty living area, where she stopped for a moment by the window. It was late afternoon. The winter sun was low in the sky, sinking gradually over a gray urban sprawl, and creating an intense coal-red glow which lit up the horizon. Below, the headlights of the rush-hour traffic were beginning to crawl past, while crowds of commuters jostled their way along the busy pavement; everyone wanted to be home before it got dark and cold. Laura felt a rush of anxiety. Her two months were up and suddenly she didn't want to lose all this. She wanted to hang onto it, keep it close, but she knew she couldn't. She turned away and headed down the hall.

In the bathroom, a painted wicker chair stood in the corner. Laura had discovered it in the hall cupboard on an earlier visit. She sat down and tipped out the contents of her carrier bag onto the floor. She checked that she had brought everything; plenty of candles of various shapes, sizes and scents, a box of matches, a packet of incense sticks with a ceramic base, luxury bubble bath and bath salts, fruit-smelling soap, some hair pins and her favourite red silk scarf. Last of all she checked her make-up; lipstick, eyeliner, eye shadow and mascara, all waterproof, all brand new just for this occasion, bought on the way.

Laura placed some of the candles around the corners of the bath, moving them about and standing back to consider them until she was happy with the way they were grouped. She placed the remaining candles around the bathroom, on the window sill, on the floor, on the sink. Next she put two of the incense sticks in the ceramic base and placed it on the shelf below the mirror. She turned on both bath taps. As the water cascaded and splashed merrily, she added the luxury bubble bath and a handful of the bath salts. When the bath was full, Laura turned the taps off and leaned over to test the water, swirling her hand around and making the bubbles dance.

She slipped off her shoes and placed them tidily under the wicker chair, and then she slowly and methodically began to undress. She folded her skirt and blouse and laid them over the back of the chair. Next she took off her tights, her bra and her underwear and laid them all on the seat. She tried not to look at her nakedness, at the scars of her recent battles with the vicious demon which was winning the war, spreading through her, eating her up, making her decide to do this.

Moving on to her next task, she stood in front of the mirror above the sink, pulled her hair up away from her face, twisted it into a ponytail and then wound the silk scarf around it, fixing it in place with the pins. Last of all she applied her new make-up. First the eyeliner, eye shadow and mascara, then the lipstick, a natural pink, not too bright. She inspected her face in the mirror, happy with the results, but unable to raise a smile.

Finally she lit the incense sticks and all the candles and turned off the light. She waited a moment and drank in the scene. The bathroom now had a mystical look, full of flickering flames and dancing shadows. She stepped carefully into the bath, lay back and stretched out. The water immediately ran in all directions around her, finding and filling every nook and cranny of her elderly worn-out shape. She lay back, closed her eyes and allowed the gentle smell of sandalwood to drift over her. She thought of all the times when a relaxing bath had put the world to rights or provided a welcome private space from her busy day.

After lying like this for a long time, deep inside a thousand thoughts and memories, the water began to turn cold.

Laura sighed heavily and came back to reality. It was time. This was the moment she'd practiced for two months. She took a deep breath, pulled her knees up towards her chin, closed her eyes and slid down below the bubbles. Above her, she sensed the surface of the water slipping and sloshing backwards and forwards before it gradually settled down again. A few strands of her hair, escaping her scarf, floated around her head like pond weed. Slowly she let out her breath and the bubbles pushed up to the surface. When the last of the air was expelled from her lungs and it was time to take another breath, she opened her mouth, immediately felt water rush in to fill the space, but it was alright. She was ready. She braced herself and breathed in hard, welcomed the silent, dreamy quality of her well-rehearsed underwater world.

*

When George got home from his business trip, he discovered the letter Laura had left for him. Bemused, he turned the enclosed door key over and over as he pondered what to do. In her letter, Laura asked him to go to an address he didn't recognize, without an explanation. Since she wasn't at home, he didn't think he had much choice, so here he was, full of trepidation, closing the door of the secret apartment behind him. He stood in the hallway, unsure about what to do next, aware of a heavy silence which unsettled him, but just then he heard a sound. He listened more carefully and heard it again, the distinct sound of gently splashing water.

"Laura?" he called, peering down the hall in the direction of the sound.

"Is that you, George?"

A smile of relief at the familiar voice.

"I'm in the bathroom, second door on the right."

George walked along to the second door and slowly pushed it open. Inside, he discovered a bathroom bathed in light. Candles of all shapes and sizes were placed along the side of the bath. More candles stood on the window sill, on the sink and across the floor. Incense sticks burnt on the shelf below the mirror. The intermittent flickering of the candle flames and the scent of the incense sticks gave the bathroom a gentle, ambient feel.

Laura was leaning back in the bath, surrounded by bubbles. Her make-up was perfect. Her hair was wrapped up in her favourite red silk scarf, the one he'd bought for her on a business trip to Hong Kong. George had always thought his wife was beautiful, but now she looked particularly beautiful in an eerie, ethereal way.

"Hey, baby. You found my note, then."

She smiled up at him.

"Yes, I did, but Laura, what are you doing here?"

She smiled again, that lovely smile.

"Taking a bath, of course."

George noticed the wicker chair in the corner. He rearranged Laura's clothes, pulled the chair up next to the bath and sat down.

"We have a perfectly good bathroom at home."

"I know, but I needed a different one."

"I don't understand."

"You don't have to."

George breathed out slowly.

"So, whose apartment is this?"

"It's mine. I rented it."

"Why?"

Laura stared into the bubbles and then looked back at her husband.

"If I tell you, promise you won't laugh."

"I promise."

Laura paused.

"I can breathe underwater," she said quietly.

George stared at his wife, intrigued and amused, and he loved her so much that he knew he couldn't help but indulge her little game.

"Really? And when did you find out you could do this?"

"About six weeks ago. I was lying in the bath…"

"This bath?"

"Yes. Anyway, I got to wondering what it would be like to slide down under the water and see if I could stay there. First time I tried, I coughed in all the bath water and had to sit up quickly, but when I practiced, I found I could stay underwater and breathe. Isn't that brilliant, George?"

"I suppose, but listen, why didn't you tell me you'd rented this place? Why did you keep it secret? And why didn't you tell me before that you could breathe under the water?"

"It wasn't the right time."

"And this is?"

Laura was suddenly serious.

"I thought you would try to stop me," she looked at George, "and I didn't want you to stop me."

"Honey, I've never stopped you doing anything. You know that."

"I know, but well, this time it's different. It's important that I can do this, something personal, just for me, something that I can control," Laura glanced down towards her naked body, hidden beneath the soapy water, before she continued, "and when I discovered I could breathe underwater, it was something special, just when I needed something special. I thought you might try to stop me, for the first time in our lives."

George looked at his wife. He said nothing, because he didn't know what to say.

"So, can I show you?"

"What – now?"

Laura nodded, but George noticed that she didn't seem so excited any more.

"Laura, I…"

"Ssh, George. Listen. Come over here and hold my hand."

Sensing the importance of the moment, George stood up, took off his heavy overcoat and hung it on the back of the bathroom door. He pulled up his trouser legs a little to give himself some slack, and knelt down carefully, bending one knee at a time against his creeping arthritis. Close up, he thought his wife was even more gorgeous. Of course he could see the reality of her – graying hair, wrinkled looks, the ravages of her recent illness - but behind that he saw her as she'd been over the years; his young wife, an excited new mother, a proud doting grandmother. All these women were there together, hiding behind the pretty eyes that looked so determinedly into his own.

Laura reached out a slippery wet hand and George took it, holding it tightly in both of his own.

"Do you know I've always loved you, George?"

"Yes, always. I never doubted. And you, Laura? You know I've always loved you, don't you?"

Laura nodded.

"That's why I want you to let me do this, OK? Don't stop me."

Tears suddenly pricked George's eyes and began to trickle down his cheek.

"No, George, no tears. I've practiced for this moment. I'm ready."

"Can I kiss you first?"

"Of course."

George leaned over and tenderly kissed his wife. As their lips met he felt the same touch, the same taste, the same smell of their first kiss all those years ago. He closed his eyes against the moment, wanting it to go on forever, but he opened them again when Laura squeezed his hand.

"So, are you watching?"

George nodded. Slowly Laura slid downwards. She held onto George's hand, keeping a loving eye contact with him until she disappeared from view. George tightened his grip - he would never let her go! – and watched as she pushed herself below the surface, as the bubbles of Laura's breath fought their way upwards, as he caught a glimpse of her hair wafting in the water, and then the bubbles stopped. George was left alone. He held onto Laura's hand and sat very still, watching the flickering candles.

*

A quiet knock made George look up. In a single sweeping glance, he saw his son-in-law pushing open the bathroom door, concern on his face, saw his daughter following behind, recoiling in horror, her hand pressed to her mouth. What was wrong? He turned back quickly, following the direction of their gaze, only realizing then that he was sitting in the dark.

The bathroom light was switched off. Everything was silent and cold. Burnt-out incense sticks, burnt-down candles, cold water, his cold hands clutching her one cold hand. Somewhere else in the apartment, he heard his daughter release a sound like an animal cry, full of anguish and pain. George looked up, unable to move.

"We got a letter and a key today, in the post," his son-in-law explained, "and we came straight over," then his voice trailed off into a sigh, "Oh, Laura!"

"But I don't understand. I was talking to her, just now."

"And I'm sure she heard you, George."

"No, listen. She was talking to me. She…" George paused, his voice choked. "She said I shouldn't try to stop her."

He felt his son-in-law's gentle hand on his shoulder.

"You can let go of her hand now, George."

George shook his head.

"George," his son-in-law whispered firmly. "Listen. We need to call for help. She's been here a while."

<u>Chapter 11</u>

The mood of Alice's event had completely changed. Now it felt heavy and dark. When George finished reading his story, everyone sat around the table in silence, then without speaking, Bill got up and stood behind George. He put a hand on his shoulder. Harry joined him and gave George's other shoulder a manly squeeze. They sat down again and while everyone watched, Babs, Daisy and Emma walked over in turn and gave George a hug.

During this show of support, George's daughter Mary had been sitting at the other end of the table, making no move to go to her father. She'd cried all the way through his reading and now it was George who got up and began to walk around the table towards her, but she got up and rushed out of the room before he could reach her. He didn't follow her.

"Er, I'll go," said Alice, although she had no idea what she was going to say. For some reason, the final story of her project had clearly brought out some raw emotions.

The evening was changing direction and she didn't feel equipped to deal with it.

She found Mary leaning against the wall, a little way down the corridor, blowing her nose into a tissue. She turned away as Alice approached.

"I'll be alright, really. I just need a minute."

"I'm sorry you're upset," Alice replied, "I feel terrible. I didn't know what George was going to write about."

Mary sighed heavily. She glanced at Alice.

"It's been such a horrible year. Mum had cancer and she decided to," Mary paused, "She did what Dad just wrote about in his story."

Alice was horrified.

"But the group agreed they would write fiction! That was the plan. Now I feel even more terrible. I'm so sorry."

"You don't need to keep apologising. Ever since we found her, and it did happen like he said, in a rented apartment, he keeps insisting that that whole episode happened, that he spoke to her before we got there."

"I don't know what to say."

"There's nothing you can say. I don't mean to be rude, but there's never anything anyone can say. It's all so final."

"And believing he had a last conversation with your Mum is your Dad's way of dealing with what happened."

"Oh, I know," said Mary, as she put her tissue away and stopped crying, "It's just seems so weird that he would do that. I mean, I just wish I could have been allowed a last chat with my Mum, but I wasn't. Dad's way has been different. He's made up a conversation that he keeps insisting really happened, instead of wishing it had and regretting it didn't, like me."

"But perhaps Alice's project has helped your Dad," said a voice behind them, "which is what I was hoping for when he asked to join the group."

Mary and Alice turned around. Maureen had left the Day Room and was walking towards them.

"Oh, Maureen, I feel so bad that my project has ended like this," said Alice, starting to well up herself. Maureen squeezed her arm gently.

"Don't feel bad. If you end up working with the elderly, Alice, you'll find that sometimes they use an unexpected opportunity to deal with something and get it out of their system. I think that's what George has done tonight, and turned a corner in his grief."

She turned to Mary now.

"As you know, Mary, we were worried when your Dad arrived because he was so quiet and so shut down about your family's experience. Writing about it in the group may have really helped him. You may find he doesn't talk any more about that conversation he believes he had with your Mum."

"I hope so. I'll go back inside. I know I should support him. It's just, when he read it out just now, it all seemed so public and invasive."

When they went back into the Day Room, they found that Babs and Daisy had taken charge of serving the last remnants of the pre-reading drinks and snacks. Mary went straight over to her father. They hugged each other and began to chat, while some of the other guests put on their coats, ready to leave. Michael picked up his jacket and helmet and walked over to Alice.

"I'm sorry I can't stay," he said, "I just stopped by on my way to my night shift. Hey, thanks for doing this for my Grandad and his friends. I think he enjoyed writing the story. He's a character, right?"

Alice laughed.

"He certainly is," she said, "Thanks for coming. I'm glad you enjoyed it."

"And you know," Michael continued, "the story Bill wrote, it really happened."

This time Alice didn't laugh. She stared at Michael.

"What do you mean?"

"It was just last year. I really did come back from travelling in Oz and found out my Dad and my uncle had restored Grandad's old bike. I brought it over here, put him in the sidecar and took him for a spin."

"And the other bike? The Triumph?"

"Yes, it turned up on our ride, just like my Grandad said. Same bike, same number plate, same hand signal before he rode off."

"But," said Alice, "was it his friend's bike? The exact same one?"

"Doubt it. Like Grandad said, his friend was killed when it was wrecked."

"But who was riding it? And how did it have the same number plate?"

"No idea," Michael grinned at Alice with the same look of mischief she saw in Bill, "Who do *you* think it was? Anyway, gotta go. I think you should definitely do another project like this, and good luck with your uni course."

Mary and Lisa followed Michael out of the door. They waved across the room at Alice, and she was glad that Mary looked a bit happier.

"Thank you for coming!" she called.

Next, Babs's son David walked over to Alice.

"Great evening, Alice. Thank you for putting it together."

"You're welcome."

There was a pause.

"Er, did you happen to know," Alice felt a little foolish, "I mean, did you already know Babs's story? Have you heard it before?"

"No, I haven't. It was a nice surprise. I mean, of course I remember when my Aunt Edie died. That wasn't that long ago. Mum used to go round a lot and cook dinner with Uncle Arthur, keep him company, until she moved in here. I know that much. She probably thought he wouldn't bother eating if he was on his own."

"Right," Alice agreed.

"She does have a very vivid imagination. Did you know she was a teacher when she was younger?"

"No, I didn't."

"Well, anyway, I'll be off. See you soon."

"Bye."

Mike approached Alice.

"Goodbye. Thanks for doing this. I liked Dad's story. I remember those winters. Long, cold and dark, but I never heard about the time they were so snowed in they couldn't get to hospital."

"And did…," Alice paused.

"Yes?"

"Oh, never mind. Thank you for coming tonight."

The Day Room Gang were gathered around the dining table and Paul, Emma's Goth grandson, was the only guest left. He hugged his grandmother and came over to Alice.

"That was great," he said, "I didn't expect the Oldies to write such interesting stories! And also, now maybe I've got an explanation."

"Oh? What for?"

"My Gran has a scar on her side, just here," he replied, indicating his own left side. "I never knew how she got it. Nobody ever said."

"Do you think the things in your Gran's story really happened?"

He looked at Alice strangely.

"When I said maybe I've got an explanation, I meant for my Gran's scar. If she was attacked in a burglary, I can understand why she or the family wouldn't ever want to talk to her grandkids about it. Hang on – you thought I meant she'd really come back from the future to save herself? Why would I jump to that conclusion? Did *you*?"

"No. It's just a feedback question for my project," Alice replied, trying to save face.

Paul headed towards the door, waving one last time and blowing a kiss to Emma, and Alice was finally left alone with the Day Room Gang. They watched her as she walked towards the dining table and sat down. At first, nobody spoke. Alice looked at Babs, then Bill, then Harry, then Daisy, George, Emma, unable to read their thoughts.

"Well," said Bill, "Did you like our stories?"

Alice paused.

"I loved your stories," she began, "They were completely different to what I was expecting, but George, is it alright if I ask you something?"

George looked at her, waiting. What was Alice hoping for with her question?

"Is your story true?"

He nodded.

"And I really, really wish it wasn't," he replied.

"Michael said something before he left," Alice said, turning to Bill.

Bill grinned across the table at her.

"Yup, my story's true."

"You went on a ride with your old friend."

"I did."

"And my story is true," said Emma.

"Mine too."

"And mine."

"And mine."

Alice waited a moment. What was the best way to proceed? What would happen if Alice said she didn't believe them?

"But we made an agreement," she said, "It had to be fiction."

"And we got together and decided to break the rule," said Daisy. "Are you angry with us?"

"No, of course not. I'm just finding it hard to believe you."

"What about?" said Bill, "That we tricked you, or that we told true stories?"

"What you wrote in the stories. I can't believe all that really happened. That seems," Alice paused, wanting to say 'ridiculous' or 'incredible', "It all just seems impossible."

"That's what I thought, until I came to live here and found that my new friends had 'experienced the impossible' in some way, just like me," said Babs. "Truth can be stranger than fiction. That's what they always say!"

"Of course they're true," said Harry, "What kind of imaginations do you think we have?"

"After all, we're elderly, remember?" said Bill, winking again.

Everyone laughed and even George raised a smile.

*

On the way out, Alice stopped by Maureen's office.

"Come in, Alice. You just caught me before I left. I switched my hours around so I could stay a bit later for your reading."

Alice sat down at Maureen's desk without speaking.

"I must say," Maureen continued, as she shuffled papers and tidied up, "I was very impressed with the stories. I tell you, that little gang, they spend hours down there in the Day Room. I guess they've fired up each other's imaginations during their little chats down there. I think this experience has been very beneficial."

She paused.

"Are you alright, Alice? You look a bit bemused."

"Yes, I'm just feeling tired, and relieved it all went well."

"And try not to worry about George and his story. I think he'll be fine. If it's alright with you and the rules of your project, perhaps you could put all the stories into a booklet and we could have a copy."

"I was going to suggest that anyway, and the stories belong to their authors, not to me. Maureen, can I ask you something?"

"Of course."

"The wife in Harry's story, Martha, that was his real wife? He wrote about her?"

"Yes. She passed away two years ago, not long after they came to live here."

"From cancer?"

"No, just from the complications of old age. Comes to us all, I'm afraid, but I know she'd had cancer treatment in the past and made a complete recovery, so that's a blessing. They had a bit more time together."

"And Daisy?"

"You know, it was so nice that she set her story in her old garden. I went there one time, to meet her and her daughter before she joined us. The house and the garden, just beautiful! She's only been here a few months. I think the corona crisis made her realise she didn't want to live on her own any more."

Maureen stood up, grabbed her bag and turned off the desk light.

"But Alice, if you don't mind and you don't need anything else, I'm off home myself."

"No, thank you," said Alice, also standing up, "I'll pop by with a booklet of the stories, and if it's alright with you, I'd like to keep in touch with the Day Room Gang."

"No problem. Pop by whenever you like. Right then, I'm off. See you soon. Have a nice evening!"

Chapter 12

Outside, the evening was crisp and dry. The sky was clear, revealing a carpet of stars, and the full moon lit up the path through the care home's landscaped garden. Alice sat down on a bench for a moment, before she headed home. She pondered on the evening's events. What was she going to write in her project report? Her tutor advice and her own research hadn't prepared her for this kind of outcome. Words such as 'evaluation', 'assessment' and 'observation' just didn't seem appropriate to Alice's experience, but how could she use 'magical', 'world-changing' and 'unbelievable' in a university report?

She thought about the stories she'd heard tonight. How could they possibly be true? Why did the Day Room Gang think they were true? Is this something she didn't understand about the elderly, that they didn't just confuse the events in their memories, but that they were also capable of inventing fantastical events and then believing they'd really happened?

She stood up, threw her rucksack over her shoulder and set off down the path. The evening was quiet. No-one else was about. Alice headed towards the little side entrance with the latched gate, which she always used because it was closer to her bus stop, when suddenly she stopped in her tracks. A shadow shot across the path ahead of her, near the gate. Alice knew immediately that it wasn't a mouse or a rat; the shape was all wrong. It wasn't a cat; it was too small. Alice hurried over to the place where the shape had disappeared into the shrubbery. She put her rucksack on the ground, knelt down and peered into the undergrowth.

Alice froze, confused and amazed at the same time, when her eyes confirmed what she thought she'd seen on the path. There, hiding behind the thick stem of a large hydrangea, was a tiny little woman, about six inches high. At first, the woman stared back at Alice from behind the shrub, then she stepped out and stood in the moonlight on the edge of the path. Her deep red hair was tied up in a bun. She was dressed in a long skirt and a jacket that were clearly cobbled together or hand-made, and which bore the dust and mud of time spent outdoors.

"Nancy?" whispered Alice.

"You know my name? But who are you?"

"You're real!"

"Of course I'm real, and I say again, who are you?"

"My name's Alice. I've been working with some of the people here at the care home. One of them is Daisy and..."

"Daisy? Oh, you saw Daisy, my Daisy. Is she alright?"

"She's fine. She wrote about you in a story."

"She did? Oh, how lovely!"

Nancy clasped her tiny hands together in glee.

"I was just looking around for a place to climb up and peep through a window, in the hope that I'd see Daisy, but whoever looks after the garden here has made it very neat and tidy. I couldn't find any way to get up to the windowsills. I'm off back to Maida Vale soon, to my other old lady, and I just wanted to make sure Daisy was happy.”

“I can help you,” said Alice. “Here, you can get into the pocket of my coat.”

“Oh, really? Thank you, Alice!”

Alice picked Nancy up and popped her into her pocket. She hurried back up the path and round the back of the care home buildings, to where the windows of the Day Room looked out over the garden.

“I don’t want Daisy to see me,” Nancy whispered, “I just want to peep in.”

Alice lifted Nancy onto the windowsill and then waited to one side, out of sight. Nancy knelt down and lifted her head over the bottom of the window frame, just enough to peep inside.

“Oh!” said Nancy, which Alice took to be a good sign.

“Can you see Daisy?” she whispered.

“Yes. She’s sitting at the table, reading. There are,” Nancy paused and counted, “five other people there.”

“They’re her friends,” Alice replied. “They spend a lot of time together.”

“And she’s happy?”

“I think so.”

"And I'm so pleased I saw her. Now, can you lift me down again, please?"

"Back into my pocket?"

"No, no, just put me on the ground. I'm off that way."

"Will you be alright?"

"I'll be fine. I've been keeping my skills sharp! Goodbye! Nice to meet you!"

And with that parting comment, Nancy waved, ran off into the shadows and disappeared. Alice watched her go and set off down the path for a second time. As she caught her bus and travelled home, she stared out of the window into the darkness, at the passing world; a world she thought she understood, but that might be filled with all sorts of wonders she hadn't even contemplated before she met the Day Room Gang.

And, she'd met Nancy, a character from Daisy's true story. Nancy was real. Would Alice ever see her again? Who knows, but it was nice to know there was a possibility. And could Alice tell anyone about her? Of course not. After all, who would believe her?

Thanks for reading! If you enjoyed this book, I'd be very grateful if you'd post a short review on Amazon. Your support really does make a difference and I read all the reviews personally.

If you would like to find out more about my writing, please go to my website: www.maggieholman.com, or my Amazon Author Page and Goodreads Author Page.

Thank you,
Maggie